She Got It Bad for a Montgomery Hitta

KEHLANI & KHALIL

By: Kelsi McMeans

D1521783

© **2019**

Published by *Miss Candice Presents*

All rights reserved.

This is a work of fiction.

Names, characters, businesses, places, events, and incidents are either the products of the author's imagination or used in a fictitious manner.

Any resemblance to actual persons, living or dead, or actual events is purely coincidental.

Unauthorized reproduction, in any manner, is prohibited.

Prologue

Trust. Something that can be easily broken but not easily earned. It's always the people closest to you that will turn on you in a blink of an eye. Never in a million years did I think I would be standing in a room with my gun drawn on two people that once meant so much to me. In this life, it was either kill or be killed, and I knew for damn sure I didn't plan on dying today.

"If you don't blow this motherfucker's head off in the next two seconds I promise you I will!!"

I stood there with my guns aimed and my hands trembling like a motherfucker as I moved. I killed motherfuckers on the daily, but right now it seemed like the hardest thing I ever had to do. I was a trained killer and the shit sort of became second nature to me.

The way the two of these motherfuckers betrayed me, there shouldn't have been a question about ending their lives.

I was riding with my nigga right or wrong, and since day one he has proven himself to be the only loyal person in my corner. So, I guess that meant I already knew what the fuck I had to do!

Without another thought, I let off a couple rounds as tears started rolling down my face, but I quickly wiped them away. There was no room for emotion in this game, you had to know how to turn that shit on and off, or you were bound to fuck up.

"Get what the fuck we came for and let's ride Lani!!"

I did what I was told, grabbed the money and the drugs and hauled ass.

Business was Business, never personal.

Chapter 1

"THE BEGINNING"

KEHLANI

"Kehlani! Kehlani! Hurry your ass up. You're going to make us miss the bus", my best friend Autumn said.

"Just chill girl, we're not going to get left, and if we do I'll make sure we get there."

"You must have a magic school bus or something because I know for damn sure there isn't a whip out in the driveway with your name on the title."

"Girl hush, and mind the business that pays you…oh, I forgot that's none." I said laughing hysterically as I put the finishing touches on my makeup.

"Let's ride bitch."

"Here your ass goes with the theatrics."

"Girl you know what the fuck I mean!"

Autumn was on my ass about getting to the bus

on time so that we could hit up the mall. She was my best friend and has been for as long as I could remember.

It took time for this beauty, and I took pride in looking good whenever I was in the public eye. You never knew who was watching and I couldn't ever be caught slipping. I wouldn't consider myself high maintenance; I just had an image to uphold.

My name is Kehlani Brooks. I'm a seventeen-year-old little baddie. I was fun size standing at 5'1. I wasn't a small chick, but I wasn't fat either. I was a borderline BBW. My breasts were a solid D cup, my waist was small, but I had an ass that you could sit a cup on. My skin was a pretty brown chestnut color. My eyes were a pretty brown color that brightened in the sunlight.

I know what you're thinking, what the hell is a seventeen-year-old doing with a body like that. Truth is I didn't know myself; I guess it just came naturally. When people looked at me, they automatically assumed that I was having sex. Truth was that I was a virgin.

My body drew all kinds of attention, some wanted, some unwanted.

I used my looks to finesse these niggas and get what I wanted from them. In reality, all they wanted was ass, so I made them believe that they had to work for it by buying me nice shit and keeping my pockets fat. I wasn't giving this nookie up anytime soon. They could erase that thought from their mental.

Autumn and I were headed to the mall to get us some bad outfits for tonight, all courtesy of Deon. Deon was somebody that was trying to be my man. He was a good-looking guy too, chocolate with pearly white teeth, but he wore pull out slugs from time to time. He wore his hair in a low brush cut. He was a little on the thick side weighing about 180 pounds. He wasn't fat; it was all muscle from him being a former football player.

He dropped out of school to make ends meet for his family. Also throwing away his potential football scholarship to Auburn University. He was talented as hell on the field, and I hate to see him let it all go down the drain. Sometimes life throws us curveballs, and it's either stands in the way and get hit or catch the motherfucker and make do with it. That was the unfortunate world we lived in.

He had been trying to get at me for a while now, and I just recently started giving him the time of day. All he wanted was for me to answer his calls and texts and let him see me whenever he wanted to, and he kept me straight. That was easy to do as long as my bitch ass foster mother didn't interfere.

Sometimes I felt like I was living in hell, and other times she simply didn't give a fuck what I did. It's like she picks and chooses when she wants to be a foster mother to me and my baby brother JJ, short for Jeremih Jr. We been with Aretha since our parents died in a hit and run accident a while back. At that time, I was eleven and JJ was six years old. Losing my parents took a toll on me for the worst, and I rebelled as a way of coping.

Eventually, I knew that they wouldn't appreciate me getting in trouble in school, so I got my act together. I had to be a role model for my baby brother, and I couldn't show him that it was okay to act out because ,he would follow in those same footsteps. I couldn't have that for either of us.

Most people would be appreciative for someone to take them in when they had no one else. Maybe I would have been if Aretha didn't see dollar signs whenever she looked at us, we were only a check to her.

The Montgomery Area Transit Bus came to a halt snapping me out of my thoughts. Autumn and I exited the bus and headed to the entrance of the mall. Our first stop was going to be Charlotte Russe. Their clothes were nice, and on the classy side, their shoes were bad as hell. Plus, I could get a full fit for $100 or less. Deon gave me enough money to splurge if I wanted to, but I had no interest in going broke as soon as I got my hands on a little money.

I just needed enough to get my gear right for this college party we were sliding through tonight. If my best friend didn't have it that was no problem; she knew I had her for whatever she needed. That's what type of friends we were; we always made sure to look out for one another.

Once we had our outfits picked out, we stopped

by the nail shop to get full sets and pedicures. We grabbed a quick bite to eat from the food court then headed to the bus stop to wait for the bus.

The bus arrived in no time, we paid our two-dollar bus fare and had a seat towards the back. We lived on the Westside, so it took us about twenty minutes to get home due to the frequent bus stops.

The day party was starting around 4:00 and it was a little after five now.

"Autumn is Shaunie still going to let us use her car tonight?"

"Yeah, she decided to swing with us tonight."

"Aww shit, it's lit then. Big sis rolling with us, so I know it's about to be a lituation"

Alabama State University was one of the hottest HBCU's in the state of Alabama, and they were known for being hype as hell. Any time they threw a party that hoe was bound to jump. We decided against the day party and tried to find another move.

We were going to the Sigma party at Club Envi but decided to go to the house party on Burton Ave instead. Since we were going there instead of the club that meant I needed to change my attire. I decided to wear an all over black spandex romper with red and yellow stripes on the side that zipped up in the front. My all-over red classic Adidas were on my feet, with a gold charmed ankle bracelet adorning my ankle.

I slicked my hair up with eco styling gel and attached a '20-inch ponytail. My brows and lashes were done so I applied my favorite lip gloss to give my lips that extra pop and I was ready to head out once I sprayed on my Gucci Bloom perfume.

Autumn wore a red t-shirt dress with red and white chucks to match. She wore her hair in a deep wave curly sew in.

The doorbell rung, and I knew it was Shaunie, so I sent Autumn to open the door. Luckily, Aretha was working a double tonight at the nursing home, so I wouldn't have to worry about her being on my ass. JJ was staying over some friend's house, so I knew that he was cool. I didn't have a thing to worry about tonight but having a good time. If JJ needed me, he knew all he had to do was hit my line, and I was there with no hesitation.

Shaunie walked in dressed to impress with her orange crop top short set that complimented her high yellow skin from being half white.

We were dressed to the T and ready to hit these gump town streets. Shaunie had a black '09 Nissan Altima with 24-inch chrome rims. We were looking good and riding good.

"Y'all smoking tonight?" Shaunie asked.

"I am," Autumn responded quickly.

"I might hit the blunt."

"Okay bet, Lani you're driving. Swing through Circle K to get some rello's," Shaunie said.

I pulled off, and we headed to the store. When we pulled up to the gas station all three of us exited the car to enter the store. I wanted a pack of Doublemint gum and a Dr. Pepper. As I was reaching in the freezer, I saw someone watching me out of my peripheral vision. When I looked up he pretended that he was occupied with his phone, I just smiled and made my way to the register.

When I got to the register Autumn, and Shaunie was already there waiting for me. As we all put our things on the counter, Mr. Mysterious showed up again.

"Aye I'm going to cover that for them," he said to the Arab cashier.

"Thank you, but we got it," I said.

"Girl let somebody do something for you," Shaunie said and I gave her a stern look that said shut the fuck up.

Our stuff didn't cost no more than $15. He handed the cashier a hot twenty and walked away without saying anything else.

At that moment I noticed how handsome he was, a pretty boy but handsome. He resembled the guy that played Ralph in the New Edition Story. He wore a cream-colored Biker Jacket with some black Ralph Lauren jeans. He wore black, grey, and white air max on his feet. Underneath his jacket, he wore a black polo v-neck shirt. A gold Rollie adorned his wrist, and he wore a gold cross around his neck. His teeth were pearly white, he had deep dimples in each of his cheeks. The man was fine as hell! I had no problem admitting that.

"Y'all know dude or something?" I asked them.

"Hell nah, but I wouldn't mind getting to know him," Autumn said, and all three of us laughed.

We gathered our belongings and left the gas station. We pulled up to Burton Ave about ten minutes later. Cars were all the way down the street, so I knew the party was already jumping. I parked Shaunie's car down the street at the Family Dollar parking lot; we were going to walk down the street to the party.

I sprayed a little more perfume on, reapplied my lip gloss as I looked in the mirror. Once I was satisfied that my face was clean we exited the car.

We proceeded to walk down the street ignoring all the 'aye lil mama's' from the bums along the way. The best thing about house parties was that they didn't check for id's and you can wear anything that you wanted. The whole purpose of it was to be comfortable and not trying to dress to impress. Even though I wasn't too worried about getting carded anyways. When we approached the house that the party was being held at we could feel the bass from the speakers in our chest.

As we entered the gate, I saw my big brother Big playing security guard. Big wasn't my blood brother, we grew up in the same neighborhood, and he always looked out for me and JJ like a big brother.

"Lani, what the hell are y'all doing here? And Shaunie you're with the shit too!" Big said.

"Chill Big, we just wanted to have a good time tonight that's all," I said.

"Y'all better not get into no shit Lani, I mean that!" he said to me.

Satisfied with his answer, I hugged him and kissed him on his cheek and walked away smiling.

The female that was searching the woman searched us for any weapons, and we were clear to go in. Once inside we stopped at the kitchen where a mini bar was set up. I asked the bartender for a blue motherfucker, Autumn had a shot of Hen, and Shaunie was on some Peach Ciroc. We had our drinks, and we were ready to get our party on.

Once the drinks started getting in our systems, we were feeling ourselves. Shaunie pulled out one of the blunts that she rolled in the car and we put it in rotation amongst the three of us. At first, the DJ was only playing trap music, and I began to wonder when he would cater to the ladies. No sooner than the thought escaped my mind, Doe B's "Standing Ovation" started blaring through the speakers. I started feeling myself instantly. The weed and the effects of the liquor had me feeling right, I started twerking to the beat, and my girls joined in.

"Pimping you is wrong, I don't wanna be right. Put that molly on your tongue, activist in my sprite."

Before we knew it, a crowd had formed around us. Normally I would care, but at this moment I didn't give a fuck. At least I wasn't embarrassing myself like some of these females in here damn near about to break their back, trying to shake a little ass. I wasn't nowhere near stiff, and neither was my girls.

When the song ended, we stopped twerking, laughing down at the moment we just had. I was laughing and talking with my girls when I noticed him again. He was standing in the corner sipping out of his double foam cup. He was staring at me like he could see through the depths of my soul. It's like he had me in a trance, I couldn't seem to break the stare. We were having a stare down from across the room. I finally broke the stare and started paying attention to my girls. Rubberband OG's "Bout That Life" started playing and everyone was rapping the lyrics when shots rang out. I scantily looked around for my girls because everything turned chaotic within a blink of an eye.

Next thing I knew Mr. Mystery man grabbed my hand pulling me towards the exit of the house. I screamed out for my girls, they informed me that they were right behind me and we kept running until we were out the house and on another street.

When we finally felt that we were out of dodge, we stopped running.

"Where are y'all parked?" he asked us.

"Over at the dollar store," I said.

"Come on I'll walk y'all to the car."

We began to walk to the car with Autumn, and Shaunie following closely behind.

"What's your name?" he asked me.

"Kehlani..yours?"

"Khalil, you do this often?"

"Do what exactly?"

"Run from stray bullets?"

"Nahhh…not at all," I said laughing.

We continued to talk, and before I knew it, we were at the car. I was enjoying Khalil's conversation and his company. Autumn and Shaunie got into the car and left us standing beside the car still talking.

He asked was it okay if we finished our conversation at a later date; I agreed and stored my number in his phone before getting into the car. I was in a daze as I smiled looking out the window like I didn't almost just get killed minutes ago.

"What the hell is up with you?" Shaunie asked as she looked at me from time to time as she drove.

"What?" I asked cluelessly.

"That nigga got you smiling like that? What the hell he been spitting to you?"

"Girl nothing, I can't smile damn."

"I guesssss."

I wasn't stunting what Shaunie's ass was talking about, it wasn't even like that. Hell, I just met dude. I didn't know shit about him, and he knew nothing about me besides my first name.

Autumn suggested we stopped by the Waffle House to get a bite to eat, and I was glad because my stomach was growling. I had no intentions on dining in so we ordered our food to go, and we headed home. I was sort of exhausted from the long day I had so I asked them to drop me off at home. I would get up with them later, all I wanted to do was take a shower, eat my food, and call it a night.

I was smelling like a whole loud pack, and I wanted to rid myself of tonight's remnants. I got out of my party clothes and got into the shower. I lathered my body with my favorite cucumber Dove Body Wash. It had the bathroom smelling lovely, and the steam from the hot shower was giving me life.

Once I finished, I moisturized my body and got into my pajama short set. I sat on my bed in Indian Style and ate my waffle and hash brown as I watched reruns of Living Single, tickled as hell like it was my first time watching the show. I was all into the show when my phone buzzed, and I noticed it was an unknown number. I opened it, and the text read *"Just making sure you and your girls made it home safely."* That made a smile creep across my face. By the message, I knew it was Khalil. I responded letting him know that we were all in safe and sound.

I liked the fact that he showed concern and for some reason, I felt that it was genuine. He and I texted until I dozed off.

I woke up to the smell of eggs and bacon, and that was strange as hell. I went into the bathroom to take a quick shower and get myself together before exiting my room. When I walked into the kitchen Mr. Fred from down the street was sitting at the table.

I guess that's why she was cooking, trying to hook him. I grabbed two pieces of bacon and a bottle of water out of the fridge. I said Good Morning to them both before leaving the house. Today was Saturday, and I didn't plan on being cooped up in the house all day. I was going to walk down the street to Autumn's house. As I was walking down the street, I noticed Autumn sitting on the porch. I joined her, and we sat on the porch talking and watching the traffic go by. We did this for hours without getting tired.

Khalil and I had been texting on and off all day. I enjoyed talking to him, and I was interested in knowing more about this mysterious man. Yesterday's events kept replaying in my head. From him buying our stuff at the store, to him attempting to save me from the gunshots at the party last night. Why would he do all of these things for a complete stranger? Nevertheless, all of it was appreciated.

A red Camaro started creeping down the street, and I immediately recognized the car to be Deon's. He stopped in front of Autumn's house, and I walked down the stairs to greet him. He rolled down the window, and I leaned inside the car, propping up on the window seal.

"What's good ma?" he asked me before planting a soft kiss on my lips.

"Not shit, just sitting here chopping it up with Autumn."

"I was just trying to see if you wanted to kick shit with me today. We can go out to eat and see a movie or something."

"I'm cool with that; I just need to go home and get myself together."

I let Autumn know that I was riding out with Deon. We left and headed for my house. I walked back into the house to see Aretha and Mr. Fred sitting on the couch giggling like little kids. I asked her if it was okay if I went out with Deon and she just waved me off. With Fred in her face, she agreed with whatever.

I changed into some high waisted distressed jeans with rips on the thighs. My shirt was a red crop top, and I wore some cute black sandals on my feet. My ponytail was still intact from the night before so applied a little edge control to slick up my baby hairs. I sprayed on my favorite Bath and Body Works perfume "A Thousand Wishes," grabbed my MK purse and I was good to go.

Deon waited outside for me in the car the entire time, not wanting to hold a conversation with Aretha and I didn't blame him at all.

Our first stop was the AMC Movie Theatre to see "Den of Thieves." I guess this was sort of like a date even though Deon didn't want to call it that. I didn't mind being seen with him in public. We weren't in a relationship or anything, but I guess he could be considered my main squeeze. I fucked with him heavy, and he looked out for me on a level that no one else did.

When we got inside of the movies, Deon asked if I wanted anything from the concession booth and I opted for some skittles and a bottle of water. I didn't want to eat too much because I knew we were going to dinner when we left.

I enjoyed the movie even though it was long as hell. O'shea Jackson Jr. made it worth my wild though. That was a fine specimen of a man.

"Did you enjoy the movie?"

"Yes, I really did. It kept me on the edge of my seat waiting to see what would happen next."

"Hell yeah, it was lit. So where are we eating at?"

"Texas Roadhouse is fine. I have a taste for some steak and those good yeast rolls."

"Texas Roadhouse it is then."

It took us a little under ten minutes to get the

restaurant from the movies. When we got there, it wasn't too packed surprisingly.

We were seated in no time, and I was happy as hell because I couldn't wait to dive into them rolls. The waitress looked very familiar to me, and she was eyeing the hell out of Deon, being all extra friendly and shit. I found it a tad bit disrespectful even if I didn't consider myself his girl. She didn't know what I was to him and if she kept this act up, I would be sure to check her ass.

"Do you need anything more sir?"

"Nah...we're good. You're dismissed," I told her, and she walked off rolling her eyes.

I don't know what the fuck she thought this was. Deon didn't say shit, he just grinned. He knew not to test my gangsta. When our food finally arrived, she sent a waiter instead; I guess she didn't want any smoke.

We ate our food and chopped it up. Besides the extra waitress, I was enjoying this night. After getting me some yeast rolls to go home, we headed out of the restaurant. I was fumbling around my purse for my phone when we were walking out the door. I looked up and looked directly into the eyes of Khalil. He threw his head up, and I just gave him an innocent smile. Luckily Deon wasn't paying any mind as he was talking to me about something I had no clue what it was about.

Deon opened the car door for me, and I got in to have a seat. He got into the driver's seat and drove off. He was taking me home because he had some moves to make. I wasn't tripping because he had shown me a great time today.

He pulled up to the front of my house and gave me a hug and kiss on the cheek before we departed ways. I walked in the house with a smile on my face, and the craziest thing was that I wasn't sure if it was from the day I had with Deon or seeing Khalil not too long ago. I went into my room, changed into my Pj's and laid back on my bed before placing my earbuds in my ear. Sevyn Streeter's "Before I Do", played in my ear while I allowed her soothing voice to take me away. I laid there listening to the song repeatedly when my phone began to ring.

Looking at the caller ID, I noticed it was Khalil. I

looked at the phone for a good ten seconds before answering. I don't know why but I was a little nervous like I felt instant butterflies thinking of his handsome face.

"Hello."

"Hey, can you talk?"

"Yeah, I can." I said laughing knowing that he was referring to seeing me with Deon earlier.

"Cool, so I need you to do me a favor."

"What's that?"

"I want you to stop whatever you're doing and take a selfie of you in your current state and send it to me." I chuckled being a little thrown off by his request.

"I'm out of my good clothes, I don't have any makeup or anything on,," I said making excuses.

"I don't care about any of that. I want to see you just like that."

Against my better judgment I did what he asked all the while still being on the phone with him. I heard his phone buzz, so I knew that he received my picture. There was complete silence on the phone for a couple of seconds, and then he spoke.

"You're gorgeous you know that."

"Thank you,," I said blushing hard as hell from the other end of the phone.

It wasn't like I had low self-esteem or anything because I knew I was a pretty ass girl. Khalil was just making me feel an unfamiliar feeling. I never had someone to make me see the confidence in my own beauty the way he just did. He let me know that I was beautiful with makeup also, but he adored my natural beauty. It was just something about the nigga that made the wheels in my head turn.

We talked on FaceTime for hours, and we got to know more about each other. We talked about family hell just life in general. He told me that he was twenty-three years old and I was a little hesitant to tell him my age, but I did. Surprisingly that didn't stop him from wanting to fuck with me, probably because my eighteenth birthday was approaching anyway.

I was enjoying our conversation and was already looking forward to talking to him more. Strangely, I was ready to see him again. We talked so long until we both dozed off on FaceTime with smiles on our faces.

Chapter 2

KHALIL

I pulled my hoodie over my head as far as it could go as I followed homeboy as he walked through the parking deck to his car. He unlocked his car door and got into the passenger seat. While he was checking his messages on the phone, I opened the back door to his car and placed my 9mm to his head. He immediately panicked and begged for his life, I snickered at the humor in it.

"Please bruh, you don't have to do this shit," he begged.

"I do. Hassan sends his regards," I said and pulled the trigger three times. Blood splattered into my face and wiped it off with the back of my hand.

I got a rush from this shit, feeling that adrenaline running through my veins hyped me up. I checked John Doe's pockets and grabbed all of the cash he had in his wallet. He carried a briefcase with him and surprisingly it was full of Benjis. I took the whole thing before exiting the car, making sure to wipe everything down. My job was to kill his ass, but no one ever said I couldn't rob him in the process. I disappeared like a thief in the night, without a trace.

I arrived home about twenty minutes later. Taking off my clothes from my hit. I went out to my back yard and threw the clothes in a tin drum, lit a match and set the clothes on fire. I watched until everything burned to a crisp before walking back into the house. I went into my bathroom and turned the shower on with the hot water to the max adding just enough cold water. I let the hot water soothe my body as the water ran down my face and my back. Ol boy begging for his life kept replaying in my head over and over as the water hit me. I shook my head to rid my mind of the thoughts.

I finished my shower and wrapped my towel around my waist. Having a seat on my chaise, shawty from the party crossed my mind. She was bad as hell, and I was surprised at how young she was. Initially, I wasn't interested in doing in jail time for fucking with a juvie, but her eighteenth birthday was approaching so shit would be straight.

She caught my eye; her beauty intrigued me. The way her skin was a warm pretty brown color, so smooth and full of melanin. When I saw her at the restaurant with that nigga, I played it cool, but an ounce of me felt a bit of jealousy. I don't know why but I did. She wasn't mines, but since I laid eyes on her, I didn't want to see her on any other niggas' arm but mines. I wasn't going to trip though because I just entered her life, dude probably been around for a while. One thing about me anything I wanted I get it, and I wanted baby girl, so it was just a matter of time before she was mine. I would play my cards right to make her fall for me.

I sent Hassan a text to let him know the job was done, and he sent a one hundred emoji back. I was burned out for the night, so I would just swing through his spot tomorrow to pick up my dough for that hit.

I guess by now you all have discovered that I was hitta. Yeah, I murked niggas for a living. I didn't choose this life, it sort of chose me. At a young age, a caught my first body and felt nothing in the process.

Not knowing that someone was watching me the entire time. When I found out that I was caught then and only then did I feel fear. That fear was from going to jail and losing my freedom. Yet, I felt nothing as I pulled the trigger.

Thinking that the older guy would turn me into the authorities, I was nervous as hell. He took me into his home and surprisingly offered me a job at the tender age of 15. He trained me how to kill and how to do it without leaving a trace. I was a hired hitman, and I had eight years in this game now that I was 23. I knew the ins' and outs' of this game, and it paid me a pretty penny too.

I was wealthy as hell, but I still chose to live in the hood. No one knew what I did for a living. For all people knew I was just another lil slanging nigga on the block. That was because I didn't showcase everything I had. Don't get me wrong a nigga was always spiffy, but at the same time, I wasn't flashy. I didn't want to walk around with a target on my back. As a cover-up, I worked at a local Foot Locker. I loved fresh kicks, and that also gave me a discount, and I had firsthand at all new releases. So yeah it all worked out perfectly for me.

I never had much family, so a nigga was a loner out here. I was an orphan, and when I was fifteen I ran away, and I've been on my own ever since. Well until I met Hassan and he gave me work. I practically raised myself, and I don't think I turned out too bad.

Most people looked at me and saw a pretty boy, but in reality, I was tougher than Teflon. I was 5'5 caramel skin tone, I wore my hair in a fade on the sides with hair on the top was usually in four braids. I had a neatly trimmed goatee. My teeth were pearly white, and I had deep dimples that would make any girl blush when I smiled. I was a handsome ass nigga, I looked like your typical ladies' man. I didn't have time to focus on bitches, my mind was always on my next target and ways to execute the hit. It was like my brain was trained to think that way; like computer software or some shit.

No female has ever held my interest longer than a couple of weeks at the most. A lot of bitches from the hood considered me 'stuck up' because I wouldn't give their asses the time of day. I didn't have time for these hood rats that didn't have shit going for them but government assistance. Without that half of their asses wouldn't be balling the way that they were. I respected a female that got out and got her shit out the mud. Not one that was always waiting on a handout. They would even be lucky if I let them suck me off, couldn't trust these hoes because they were always looking for their next come up. I didn't need that type of energy within my proximity.

Khalani gave me a different vibe though. I think her young innocence is what attracted me to her the most. Even though she possessed the body of a grown woman, I could still tell that she had milk on her tongue. I knew I wasn't that much older than her in age, but I've been an adult since I was fifteen. I've experienced all types of shit at an early age; there wasn't nothing that I haven't seen. Sometimes life makes you grow up before time, and that was my circumstance. I don't regret any of it though because it all has made me the man that I am today. I'm stronger and wiser now.

Knowing what I did for a living and the

dangerous life I lived it made part of me want to let shorty be, but I couldn't. I wanted her in my life to add to me. I wasn't going to let her slip through my grasp that easily. It was a reason for me running in to her twice in one night.

When I saw her, I was stunned by her beauty. It wasn't shit for me to buy their stuff. I just wanted to be kind because I was checking for shorty. By the way, she tried to shut me down ,I knew that she had her own and didn't need nothing from a nigga. I liked that, but as she found out, I wasn't a nigga that took no for an answer. I paid for that shit without giving her the option to refuse my offer again.

I laughed like hell on the way to my car because I knew that probably fucked with her ego. I knew that even a gesture that small I would leave a lasting impression on her; that was my goal. Running into her again at the party had me feeling like it was fate. Like the universe was trying to push us to be in one another's presence or something. When the niggas started firing off shots my first instinct was to grab shorty. It was strange as hell, but I wanted to ensure her safety. It felt like it was my responsibility and it was one I honestly didn't mind having. I went to sleep with shorty on my mind.

After taking a shower, I got dressed in my black and red Nike windbreaker jumpsuit with black and red air force ones on my feet. I put my diamond earrings in my ear, sprayed on my Versace Blue cologne, put my black Nike fitted cap on and turned it to the back. I tucked my glock in the back of my pants before placing my jacket over it and left the house.

I got into my 2018 metallic blue Dodge Charger and headed in the direction of Hassan's spot. I was riding down the long ass road that leds to his Mansion, and it took me ten minutes to get there. No matter how many times I came through the ride never seemed shorter. As I made it to the gate, the guard noticed it was me and he let me through. I made it to the front of the Mansion and walked up the stairs to ring the buzzer.

The maid came on asking who it was, and I gave her my name, and they let me in. I waited in the foyer before the maid let me know it was okay to go back. I walked the long hallway leading to Hassan's man cave. Gave the door a light knock before walking into the study.

"What's up young blood?"

"Nothing much, shit I'm off from my other job, so I guess today will be a chill day for me."

"Ain't shit wrong with that, your ass is always working 24/7 anyways, take some time for yourself. Hell, you have enough money take or trip or something." Hassan said as he handed me the duffle bag full of money for last night's hit.

I never really thought about going out of town or anything until he just suggested it. It didn't sound like a bad idea at all, especially if I had Khalani's badass with me.

"I'm going to give it some thought," I said as I dapped him up and proceeded to leave.

I went home and split my money up into two different safes to ensure the safety of it. I sat on the couch and kicked my feet up on the coffee table as I scrolled to shorty's name in my phone. I wanted to call her, but I realized the time and figured she was still in class, so I didn't bother. I decided to do her a better one instead, and I would pull up on her at Jefferson Davis High School. I tapped my pockets to make sure I had everything I needed before leaving the house again.

I pulled up to the school and parked my car in the cut, not wanting to be too noticeable but in good enough view so I could spot her out in the crowd. I sat there waiting for the bell to ring before getting out of the car. I got out and sat on the hood of my car waiting to see her. Her friend Autumn spotted me before she did, and her face lit up like Christmas and mine did as well at the sight of her.

"Hey Khalil, what are you're doing here?" she asked me.

"Hey Autumn," I said before turning my attention back to Lani.

Placing her hand into mine, I said to her "I came to see you, take a ride with me."

"I would, but I can't leave Autumn," she said looking over at her friend.

"You don't have to leave her, we can drop her off."

She agreed knowing that her friend could ride with us. I asked if they were hungry and I'm sure they were because the schoolhouse food was never hitting on shit. We went to Five Guys, I handed Lani a fifty-dollar bill and told her to get whatever they wanted. She tried to give me my change back when she got into the car and I just slightly pushed her hand away and she stuffed the money in her purse. We dropped her friend off, and we kept riding and talking. I didn't care to keep driving so I asked if she was comfortable coming to my house and she said that it was cool, so we headed to the crib.

I lived in the hood, but my house was nice as hell on the inside, with your regular brick layout on the outside. My walls were a nice cream color, and my furniture was black, smoky grey, with a touch of red. I was a lover of art, so I had some of the most famous painters work on my walls. I could tell she was pleased with my décor the way she admired everything.

"So, your lady fixed your crib up huh? Shit's nice, I can't lie," she said as she continued to walk around checking out everything.

"What lady?" I said kicking my feet up on the coffee table.

"So, you mean to tell me that a woman didn't decorate for you?"

"Nah, I did this shit by my lonely. What you never met a nigga with good taste or something?"

"It's not that; excuse me for misjudging your taste. You have it decked out in here. I'm feeling your interior decorating skills," she said, and I chuckled at her humor.

Shorty was funny as hell, and I liked the fact that she could make me laugh. She joined me on the couch, and we continued our conversation. She inquired again about my woman, and I let her know that I didn't have one. I could tell that she didn't believe me, but I was keeping it a stack with her. I had no reason to lie about shit, I was a grown ass man, and I handled myself accordingly. If I so happened to have a woman and I wanted to fuck with another female, she would know about my lady. I wouldn't have her going in blind like that.

"Since we're acquiring about my relationship

status, what's up with you and dude from the restaurant?"

"He is somebody I've been knowing for a while, he's not my man, but he looks out for me you know?"

"Hmph, let him know that he could go ahead and resign. I'll fill that position. Whatever you need I got you."

"Just like that huh?"

"Just like that." I said, but I knew she didn't take me serious but soon she would.

I told her that I was going out of town for the weekend and I asked if she would like to join me. She said that she would have to figure out what to tell her foster mother, but she would love to go.

I was excited that she even agreed to go. That would make the little getaway worth wild. She wouldn't have to worry about anything but sitting back and looking pretty.

***

The day had finally come for us to skip town for a little while. She texted me to let me know that everything was a go. I didn't know what kind of lie she made up for her foster mother, but I was just glad she would be joining me.

I was waiting outside of her school to pick her up. This has sort of become a routine, ever since that first day, I picked her and her friend up from school. The bell started to ring and shortly after I saw her and her girl walk out of school. She made her way to me with a smile on her face, and I wore one on my face as well. As she approached the car, I met her on the passenger side of the car. I grabbed her book bag from her before placing a kiss on her cheek, and opening the door for her to enter.

I threw her book bag in the trunk while she said her goodbyes to her friend. I could have sworn I saw a look of envy on Autumn's face, but I dismissed the thought. Once they were done talking, I pulled off and headed towards I-65 south.

"Khalil, we're leaving already? I don't have any clothes or anything," she said to me.

"Baby you're with me, I got you. You don't have to worry about anything," I said as I rubbed the back of my hand against her face very gently.

She eventually became at ease, and we hit the road. I had one hand on the wheel and one hand intertwined with hers. I had the windows rolled up tight, with the sunroof back.

We made it to Destin, FL almost three hours later. She wore a big smile on her face as she checked out her surroundings. I take it shorty has never been out of the state. I was happy to be the one to show her something new.

Before checking into our beach house, I took her on a little shopping spree to get everything she needed to be comfortable during her stay. We went to the Tanger Outlets and the shopping mall. At first, she was a little hesitant as she started to pick up things, but I assured her that she was good to get everything she needed.

She looked like a kid in a candy store as she weighed me down with bags. I told her to get everything she needed, so I wasn't tripping. I picked up a couple of things for myself, and we were finally done shopping.

I reserved a nice beach house that had an amazing view on the ocean. The house had two bedrooms in each. I didn't want to crowd shorty's space if she wasn't that comfortable with me just yet. I definitely didn't want to run her off so soon. I wanted her to be as comfortable as possible.

The house was nice as hell, and it was decorated closely to my taste. So I was sure that she would love the place. I grabbed all of the bags out of the car and walked to the entrance of the house. I had her grab out of my pocket to open the house door. She walked in first, and I could tell by the expression on her face that she was pleased with the appearance of the house. I put the bags down on the table and when I turned around Kehlani lips met mine. She gave me a sweet subtle kiss on the lips.

"What was that for?"

"Just because," she said walking away smiling.

This trip has already been a good one, and we just got here. I would be sure to thank Hassan for encouraging me to take some time off and do something for myself.

Chapter 3

DEON

I had been out on the block all day, all week rather. I'd been so busy to the point I haven't made time to fuck with Lani. I was sure she was feeling some type of way by now because she hasn't heard from me. I don't mean to neglect her, but money calls and she likes nice shit. That's why I hug the block from sun up to sun down. Day in and out, hustling was all I knew.

I haven't seen her since our little outing, and I haven't talked to her since the day after. I hit her up twice today and have yet to get a response. That was strange as hell for Lani. She has always been a quick texter unless she was doing something, but she always got back with me in under ten minutes. I made a mental note to swing through the hood to see if she was out. It was the weekend, so I was sure her and Autumn was probably sitting on the porch.

"20…30…40…50." I repeatedly counted the

money over and over and each time I counted the shit still came up short.

Before I knew it, I lost all of my marbles and started beating the shit out of ol' boy. I played about a lot of things, but my money wasn't one. Shit was too hard to come by for someone to fuck with mine.

I jacked the little corner boy up by his shirt and pinned him up against the brick wall.

"You have until midnight to pay me my money in full and not a motherfucking second later!!!" I said through gritted teeth. I slung his ass away from the wall, and he walked away swiftly; practically running.

He pissed me off just that fast. I put my blunt between my lips, fired it up, and took a long pull from it. If that fuck boy didn't have my money, there was going to be hell to pay. One for playing with my money and two for wasting my time.

I had enough of this scene, so I got in my car and left the block. I reached out to Lani once more before turning on her street. She still didn't pick up.

"Hey, it's Lani, sorry I can't get to the phone right now. Leave me a message, and I'll hit you back."

My muscles tightened in my jaw as I listened to her voicemail. I ended the call without leaving a message, frustrated as hell. I turned on her street and stopped when I was in front of Autumn's house. I parked my car and rolled down the window.

"Yo Autumn, let me holla at you," I yelled out of the window. She immediately came prancing down the stairs.

"Hey Deon," she said in an overly friendly voice.

"Yo, where Lani at? I've been trying to reach her and can't seem to get up with her"

"Oh, she didn't tell you that she was going out of town with her little boo."

I felt my blood boiling, and I was getting angrier by the second. She wasn't answering for me because she was getting cozy with the next nigga. All I could imagine was him getting between her thighs. Being the first one inside of her sacred place. I shouldn't be thinking that way, but I was. Granted I never claimed her as my woman, but I honestly did see her that way. I never really told her my true feelings; I just felt like she automatically knew by my actions. I gave her anything that she asked for; she didn't have to want for shit.

True enough I did fuck with other bitch's from time to time, she was who I wanted. I knew that hella' niggas were at her, but she always kept them on the back burner, and I was always on the forefront. Well up until now, she had this new nigga that was taking her out of town and shit. I was going to find out who the nigga was if that was the last thing I did.

Autumn was still going on and on about the situation, and quite frankly I had grown irritated with her. What type of friend was she to be ratting her best friend out like that? If anybody knew how tight their relationship was it was me. They have been best friends since our elementary days. I also knew that anytime I gave her money she always made sure Autumn was straight too, couldn't put shit past these shysty bitches.

I already smoked the blunt that I had on the way over so I was preparing myself to roll up another one. With all of this shit on my mental I needed something to smoke to relieve me from these thoughts momentarily. I pulled the weed from my pocket and then reached into my dashboard for a White Owl Cigar.

Autumn saw what was about to take place, so she invited herself into my car. I just looked at her; I didn't have the energy nor the time to argue with her ass right now.

I rolled three blunts, and we were now on our second one. I was in a daze as I threw my head back and blew O's from my mouth. The next thing I knew, Autumn started fumbling with my belt.

"Aye man, what type of shit you on?!"

"Just chill. Let me take care of you. Kehlani doesn't know what to do with a nigga like you. Hell, she's taking you for granted...that nigga is probably digging in her guts right now."

She definitely knew what to say to piss me off even more. Next thing I knew her full juicy lips like Topanga was wrapped around my thick mushroom head. I started to squirm and push her head away like a little bitch, in an effort to decline her offer. I just couldn't turn her away, the warmth of her mouth felt too good. My dick came to life within seconds. Shorty engulfed the whole nine-inch curve dick into her mouth with ease.

Part of me knew that this shit was wrong, but at the same time I couldn't make myself care. I didn't know what the fuck Lani was doing with that nigga. Shit, Autumn was right, she didn't appreciate me. All the shit I've done for her, and she didn't even have the decency to tell me that she was even entertaining another nigga.

Felling myself get angrier I began to fuck Autumn's face as I grabbed on to her Brazilian weave very tightly. Within seconds I released my kids down her throat, and she swallowed every bit of it. She wiped her mouth with the back of her hand and got up with a grin on her face. I just shook my head because shorty was on some wild shit. She just gave me dome in front of her mother's house in broad daylight. We finished the last blunt, but Lani was still on my mind. I would see her soon though.

Chapter 4

KEHLANI

I was having the time of my life in Florida. Khalil was showing me such a good time and spoiling the hell out of me. I was loving every minute of it.

We went to the Big Kahuna waterpark and had a blast on the waterslides. I was surprised that Khalil was doing all of this. We were acting like two big kids, but we were having so much fun.

We were now at the Track racing on the go-karts. This trip was much needed, and I'm glad he asked me to go. Surprisingly when I asked to go out of town with a friend, Aretha just agreed with no questions asked. She was so far up Fred's ass she didn't have time to worry about me and JJ. I wasn't tripping though because I was able to enjoy my little getaway in peace with the exception of Deon blowing me up all of a sudden.

I haven't heard from him since that night we

went out. I guess he must have caught a whiff that I wasn't in the city. I put him on hide alerts, but he kept calling. I didn't want to ruin the mood, so I blocked him for the time being. I was enjoying myself, and I wasn't going to let anyone mess that up.

Our little vacay was coming to an end, and I hated to go back to Alabama. Khalil wanted to take me out for dinner, but I insisted on cooking since we were in this nice ass beach house. The kitchen was big as hell, and I could see myself moving around in it.

"Are you sure you can cook shorty?"

"Hell yeah, I can cook, don't underestimate me now. Just take me to get some groceries," I said laughing.

We went to Walmart to get a few groceries. We were leaving tomorrow, so we didn't need too much. When we arrived back at the house I asked Khalil to just sit back and relax, he did as he was asked, and I went into the kitchen to do my thing.

I was preparing a well-cooked salmon seasoned to perfection with a splash of lemon juice. Sautéed asparagus with brown rice. I fixed Khalil's food and cut a lemon to put on top of the salmon. The plate looked like something from a five-star restaurant.

I went into the living room and handed Khalil his plate.

"Damn ma, this shit looks good as hell."

"It is, try it out."

He cut a piece of salmon and placed it in his mouth using his fork. He gave me a look of satisfaction as he ate and I just smiled a cocky grin. The food was delicious if I had to say so myself.

Once we were done eating, we played a few card games. I beat him in a round of Uno and spades. But I honestly think that he was just trying to take it easy on me. After we were done playing games, we started watching TV. I cuddled up close to him, and he wrapped his arms around me, after asking if it was okay first.

I don't know what it was and I really couldn't explain it. I instantly felt comfortable when I was with him. It always made me feel good just to be in his arms. Whenever I was in his arms, I felt a sense of protection. I feel safe, and I knew that he wouldn't let any harm come my way.

Before I knew it, I dozed off as he held me and watched TV. When I woke up from my nap, it was a little after midnight. When I no longer could feel Khalil's presence, I got up. He stretched me out on the couch and placed a cover on me. The kind gesture put an instant smile on my face. This man was making me fall for him, and I was beginning to understand just what SWV talked about in their song "Weak."

I got up from the couch and made my way to the room where Khalil was sleeping. I stood in the doorway of the room as I just watched him sleep so peacefully. He was so handsome even when he was asleep. I walked over and got in the bed with him and wrapped his arms around me before pulling the covers on me. He pulled me in closer to me and held me tight before placing a sweet kiss on my back. That put a smile on my face, and we went back to sleep.

***

We were back in Montgomery, and I hate that our trip went by so fast. Just thinking back on the last couple of days we spent together made me feel butterflies inside. Khalil made it so easy for me to fall for him. The man held me tight all night and didn't try anything, and that made my respect level for him go up even more. He always showed me the utmost respect. We spooned the entire night, so I knew that it was tempting as hell for my ass to be touching his crotch. Hell, it was even tempting for my virgin Mary ass. I started to feel a tingle between my thighs every time I felt his hardness touch my ass or we brushed up against one another in a very sexual manner. That was an unfamiliar feeling for me, and it took everything in me to not calm down that urge.

Khalil was sexy as hell, and my hormones always arise when I was in his presence. Especially, now that our relationship is growing and we're becoming closer every day. I don't know if I'll be able to control it if we continue to be up under each other so much. One thing that I loved about our relationship is that we have a friendship. I can talk to him about anything, and he always would show genuine interest. It was to the point where he would confide in me and ask me for advice when he needed to make decisions. I was young, but I was wise beyond my years, I always have been. I couldn't wait to be in his presence again. There was a knock on the door and in walked my baby brother.

"What's up knucklehead, I missed you these last couple of days."

"Yeah, I bet," he said in a sarcastic tone with a smile on his face.

"No, seriously JJ I did."

"Yeah, yeah, yeah. So, who is this guy anyway?"

"His name is Khalil, he's so good to me JJ. I feel myself falling for him more and more every day, and it scares the shit out of me. I never had someone to make me feel the way he does."

"Not even Deon?"

"Not even. Deon has been around for a long time, but even he never gave me this feeling. I want something real, and I know that I'm not the only one in his life. Granted he has always looked out for me, but I don't know this was just different."

"I hear you, sis just be careful with your heart. Everyone doesn't deserve that from you."

I just sat there pondering on what my baby brother just said to me.

I knew that I was capable of loving someone wholeheartedly, I just needed assurance that if I were to give out that type of love that same unconditional love would be reciprocated back to me. By the way, things were going with Khalil and me. Soon we would be in a relationship if he asked of course. I knew that he was feeling me, and I was feeling him too.

I know sooner or later, I would run into Deon, but I would cross that bridge when it got here.

I was laying across my bed when Autumn busted into my room.

"Girl what the hell, you can't knock," I said playfully.

"Your ass didn't tell me you was back; I had to hear it from JJ."

"Get out your damn feelings, I was just trying to get some rest. I haven't talked to anybody besides my brother and Khalil."

"Umph!" Was all she said before inquiring about our trip.

Just the mention of Khalil's name made my heart flutter, and I started to blush. I filled her in on our weekend and all of the fun we had over the course of a few days. She looked around my room at all of the shopping bags on my floor that I didn't get to put up yet. She stuck her nose up in the air like she was on some jealous shit, but I paid her ass no mind. I didn't have time for no overly jealous type shit.

I didn't mean to be rude, but I told her that I would fuck with her later. She got up and left immediately. I didn't have time for any negative energy right now. I was in a good ass mood, and she wasn't going to ruin it with her negative vibes. I just wasn't feeling it right now.

Khalil was at work, but he was texting me the entire time. I was missing him like crazy. I couldn't wait for him to get off so I could see his handsome face.

I had been in my room all day binge-watching 'The Originals' on Netflix. I had my snacks in the room with me, so I didn't have to leave out. Just as I was getting all into the two brothers, Klaus and E'Lijah fuck some people up the doorbell started to ring.

I stood up from the bed still watching the TV, and it ringed again. I paused the TV, grabbed my phone, and went into the living room to see who was at the door. Looking through the peephole, I noticed that it was Mr. Fred so I opened the door and he stepped in.

"Hey, Mr. Fred, how are you?"

"I'm good Kehlani, is Aretha here?"

"She's at work actually, but I'll be sure to inform her that you stopped by," I said as I opened the door for him. He came up behind me with his tall frame covering my shadow and slammed the door shut.

"It's good that she isn't here, now we finally have our chance to be alone. I see the way that you look at me," he said as he walked towards me with lust in his eyes and it terrified me.

"The way you prance through here all of the time looking all sexy trying to get my attention, you got it. So, let me get a taste of it. These little niggas don't know what to do with you," he said as he pushed me back on the couch forcefully.

I tried using all of my strength to break through his grasp. He snatched my cami off in one whiff. Tears steadily rolled down my eyes as I realized that I wasn't strong enough to get out of this situation.

He unbuckled his pants and let them fall to his ankles. He yanked my shorts off revealing my boy shorts. I cried, begged, and screamed, and it all fell on deaf ears. I just couldn't understand what I ever did to deserve this. All of the allegations he was making were the furthest thing from the truth. I wasn't in the least bit attracted to him or trying to do things to get his attention.

He pulled his little wrinkled up sausage through the hole of his boxers. I just closed my eyes and prayed as tears continuously filled my eyes. I couldn't mentally or physically prepare myself for what was about to take place.

I heard someone fumbling with the door, but Fred continued to touch my body with his filthy hands and continued to plant sloppy wet kisses all over me. Breathing hard all into my face with his breath smelling like he just got done eating Vienna sausages and crackers. I was disgusted, to say the least. I guess his old deaf ass couldn't hear the fumbling at the door.

The next thing I knew Khalil broke into the house, damn near taking the door off of the hinges in the process. He immediately pulled Fred off of me and repeatedly threw blows in his face. He was beating the man senseless, and I didn't have an ounce of sympathy for his old perverted ass. The man was every bit of sixty years old and trying to take my innocence away from me. This world was full of sick motherfuckers like him, and there was a special place designed for them.

I went into my room to put some clothes on really fast so that I wasn't standing there in my nakedness. I threw a pair of sweatpants and an old family reunion t-shirt on quickly. As I was leaving out of my room, I could still hear them tussling.

I was so grateful that Khalil saved me from the horrifying event that was about to take place. Fred didn't succeed, but that didn't change the fact that he attempted. I became infuriated more and more, and I couldn't hold back the tears. I was beyond angry.

I went into Aretha's room closet and grabbed

her pistol out of the shoe box. I could hear Khalil talking from the living room.

"Oh, cat got your tongue now? Your ass wasn't so shy when your old ass was pushing up on my woman."

I stood in the hallway as I watched Fred beg and plead for his life the same way I begged him to get off of me not too long ago. Now the shoe was on the other foot, but the only difference was that Khalil had a gun trained on him.

"Please man, you don't have to do this. I wasn't going to do anything to her, I promise. Even though she wanted me to."

I stood there in the hallway as I listened to this man lie about me wanting that for him. I knew that Khalil wouldn't believe that shit he just spit out of his mouth.

My hands were sweating and trembling as I held the gun in my hand. My eyes were bloodshot red, my hair was distraught. I was so mad I could spit fire.

Just as Khalil was getting ready to pull the trigger, I came up from behind him and sent one shot off in Fred's stomach and then one straight to his dome.

Khalil just looked back in amazement. Tears were rolling down my face, but I felt nothing. I was numb. I just stood there, unable to move my feet. He pulled me in tightly and embraced me. He tilted my head up and kissed me ever so gently.

"As long as there is breath in my body I would never let anyone hurt you. I'm your protector, as your man that's my job."

"My man huh?" I said as I wiped the tears from my eyes, chuckling a little.

"Yes ma, let me be the man to take care of you. I promise to keep a smile on your face and bring joy into your life. From this day forward, it's me and you. We're riding until the wheels fall off."

"I like the sound of that, but Khalil how did you know what was going on?"

"I guess you butt-dialed me ma, I heard everything. I was on my way over to surprise you since I got off early."

All I could do was look up, and mouth. Thank You. Khalil was right on time like a guardian angel. He was my good luck charm.

We were so wrapped up in our conversation when JJ ran into the house yelling "what the fuck?"

"What happened Lani?"

"Fred ass tried to rape me, and I killed him JJ."

"I'm sorry y'all but there is no time to sit here and ponder on this. We have to dispose of this body. Lani pack a bag or two as quick as you can, you're coming with me. Bruh, help me get this nigga out the house," Khalil said.

I did as I was told and packed as much as I could, and went outside to wait in the car. I don't know what him and JJ were doing with the body, I was just grateful that I didn't have to be involved in this part.

I was very grateful that Khalil came when he did. I would never be able to forget what almost happened to me.

On this night a killer was born.

Chapter 5

KHALIL

I got off from Foot Locker earlier than I expected. Lani wasn't expecting me to be off until 9:00. I was going to pop up on her and surprise her. I was riding down the boulevard when my phone started to ring, and it was her. I answered immediately anxious to hear her voice after being apart from her for hours.

What I heard on the other end of the phone instantly made my blood boil.

"The way you prance through here all of the time looking all sexy trying to get my attention, you got it. So, let me get a taste of it. These little niggas don't know what to do with you."

I became infuriated as I drove my car like a maniac trying to get to Lani. I had one thing on my mind, and that was murder. I made it to their house in five minutes because I did the dash the whole way there. I pulled into their driveway damn near running my car into their house, almost forgetting to put the bitch in park. I jumped out fast as hell trying to get to the door. When I turned the doorknob, it was locked, so I kept on yanking it until it became loose and I pushed the door in.

I got in the house in enough time to see the sick bastard on top of her. I yanked his old ass off her with the quickness, holding him up by his shirt. I beat his face in bruising my knuckles in the process, but I didn't give a fuck. He would pay for fucking with mine.

His lightweight elderly frame wasn't a match for me. Even though I wasn't the biggest nigga out here, I could damn sure hold my own.

I beat that nigga until I was tired. He begged and pleaded for his life. It's funny that he thought that I would give a fuck when he ignored Lani cries and continued to try to take advantage of her. He had fucked up in a major way, but I was sure by now he has realized that. Khalil Jacobs was not the man to be fucked with, and now that Lani was associated with me, neither was she.

I already had plans of ending his life, I just

wanted to put a hurting on his ass first. After listening to him beg over and over again and continue to make false allegations against my girl I grew tired, and my trigger finger was getting itchy. I pulled my gun from my pants and aimed it at him and all of the sudden he was speechless. I chuckled in amazement.

"Cat got your tongue huh?" He couldn't say shit.

I was done fooling around with his ass. Normally I would end a motherfucker's life with the quickness. But this situation was different, it was personal. I was acting purely out of emotion. At that moment I realized just how much Kehlani meant to me. There wasn't nothing that I wouldn't do for her.

Just as I was getting ready to pull the trigger on the nigga, two shots rang out behind me. The first one hit him in the stomach, and the next one went into his head. I turned around to see Lani as the shooter. There was nothing but hurt in her eyes. I know that she probably hate that she had to do that, but it had to be done. Quite frankly, he got just what he had coming to him. That muthefucker deserved to meet his maker, hell he didn't have too much longer anyway. She just sent him on an early vacation to hell.

I pulled her in close to me to try my best to console her. After I calmed her down her brother walked in. We explained the situation to him, and he and I got rid of the body. We straightened the place up the best we could to make it seem like a robbery instead of a homicide.

Lani had her bags packed and ready to go. I told JJ that he could stay with us tonight if he'd like and he agreed so that he could be close to his sister, knowing what she just experienced. I could tell that they were tight as hell. When she told him what had transpired no further questions had to be asked. I liked that about him, he was a young nigga, but he had character.

When we arrived at my crib, I followed Lani in the room with her stuff and then gave her a little space. I went into the kitchen to get an ice bowl for my hand and poured me a glass of Henny. I threw it right back as I stood at the countertop in deep thought.

JJ walked in and thanked me for being there for his sister. I let him know that as me trying to be her man it was my duty to protect her and keep her out of harm's way.

"I would never let anyone hurt her, and I would take the last breath in my body to protect her. That's my word," I told him, and I meant every word.

From this day forward, she could count on her nigga to be by her side through whatever. I showed him to the guest room and told him to make himself comfortable. I walked into the room where Lani was and saw her sitting on the bed with her legs to her chest with tears rolling down her face. I knew that she was hurting. I just sat next to her not knowing what to say to help ease her pain.

"Even though he didn't have the chance to go through with it...I just feel nasty Khalil," she spoke barely above a whisper.

"Don't feel that way because you're not, that nigga was. You won't ever have to worry about him anymore."

I left her sitting on the bed as I went into the bathroom. I ran her a warm bubble bath with a little Epsom salt. I went into the room, and she was still in the same position I left her. I picked her up and placed her on the edge of the bed. I lifted her shirt above her head, unsnapped her bra from the back. I took off her jogging pants and then her underwear. By now she was fully naked. I scooped her up in my arms the same way a groom carries his wife over the threshold and carried her into the bathroom. Beforehand I asked her was it okay, and she assured me that it was.

I gently placed her body in the tub of water. I handled her with so much care as if she was a newborn baby. I needed her to know that she was delicate as hell because to me she was. She breathed a sigh of relief, and I knew then that the water was soothing her body. All I wanted was for her to be at peace and to relax her mind.

I lathered the bath rag and began to bathe her body with it. She relaxed more and more and just laid her back on the tub as I completed my job.

Once I finished, I noticed that she had fallen asleep. I lifted her out of the tub, dried her body off, before moisturizing her skin with shea butter body cream. I found her some underwear, shorts, and shirt out of the bag and dressed her.

I couldn't help but admire her body. Her beautiful coke bottle frame, with a little pudge, had a nigga in a daze, and I could feel my man waking up. It wasn't time for that, so I calmed myself down. I placed her in the bed and pulled the covers up on her, shortly after I joined her. I laid down next to her watching TV before I eventually dozed off.

I was awakened to Kehlani rubbing her soft hand on my chest and abs while planting soft, gentle kisses on my face. When I turned to face her our lips met and instinctively we started kissing very sensually. So passionate that I felt a bolt of electricity shoot through me. My heart was beating a mile a minute.

She had me feeling like I was in middle school all over again, experiencing puppy love for the first time. As we continued to kiss the passion turned into hunger. As I hungrily kissed her sticking my tongue in her mouth, making our tongues dance. I stroked her hair as I kissed her.

We were laying on our sides, and our bodies started to collide. She started rubbing her pelvic area against mine, and it was driving me crazy. My dick was screaming for relief as it was threatening to burst out of my briefs. I guess she felt it because she reached down and started rubbing it. I started rubbing all over her body and squeezing her breasts as we still kissed. She started grabbing on my gym shorts in an effort to get them off. I assisted her in getting them off, I was now only in my boxer briefs.

I lifted her arms up and took her shirt off, and her chest was heaving up and down. I just stared into her beautiful brown eyes, getting lost in them.

"Lani, are you sure you want to do this. I don't want you thinking this is what you want knowing what you just experienced. I don't want you to have any regrets if we do this."

"I want to Khalil, you've shown me that you care for me unconditionally. I've never been shown that type of love before. When I'm with you a feeling of true love takes over my body, and I just become weak. I want my first time to be with someone I love and someone who loves me as well. I love you, Khalil."

"I Love you Kehlani, and I realized how much tonight when everything happened. It just something about you that makes my heart melt. The sight of you leaves me breathless, and whenever I'm in your presence, I'm as nervous as I was the first time I met you. I've never felt the way I feel about you with no one else before. I know it's only been a couple of months but what I feel for you is real, there is no denying that. One thing I know to be true is that when it's real you know it, and I believe that you're my one true love, Lani."

A lone tear escaped from her eyes, but she was smiling. She kissed me and removed my briefs, and I then removed her shorts. She was wearing some candy red boy shorts, and she was looking good as hell in them. I positioned myself at her feet as she laid down. I placed her feet in my hands and started sucking on her pretty pedicured toes one by one. Once I was done with them, I started planting kisses from her feet all the way up her thighs. I could hear soft moans escaping her mouth, and I was enjoying it. Her freshly waxed pussy just stared at me, I used my hand to rub up and down her clit, and I felt her body tense up a little at my touch.

"I got you ma, I won't hurt you." I said to her in

a real sexy manner before licking my full lips.

I used one finger to open her up, gently sticking my finger inside of her honey cave. I was extra careful with her, I didn't want to hurt her in any kind of way. When I pulled the finger out it was covered in her white cream. I put my finger in my mouth and licked it all off. I proceeded to stick that same finger inside of her joined with another. Pulling them in and out slowly to get her just how I wanted her. I could feel how tight she was by how difficult it was to get my two fingers in. I could only imagine how I would get this thing between my legs inside of her.

"Open it up for me." I said to her as I place her hand on her pussy lips to spread them apart, so I could have full access to her clit. I positioned myself between her legs as I laid on my stomach to get eye level with it. I could see it just glistening at me, but it still wasn't exactly how I needed it to be. I wanted her to be as wet as a Tsunami, dripping like a faucet. Yeah, I was a nasty nigga, and by the time I was done with her, my face would be covered with her juices like I just got done eating a watermelon down to its rind.

I used my tongue to lick up and down her clit very slowly but sensual. I used my lips to slurp on her clit while my tongue massaged it. While I did that, I stuck two fingers inside of her simultaneously. It was driving her crazy, and her moans was all of the encouragement a nigga ever needed.

"You like that shit?"

"Yeahhhh."

"It's good?"

"How good?"

"Real gooood," she moaned out in ecstasy not being able to control the nut I was making her bust.

"Tell me you like it, Lani."

"I like itttttttt, Khalil what are you doing to me?"

"Giving you everything your heart desires baby," I said between slurps.

I began to stick my tongue in and out of her repeatedly, and it drove her wild. I put my whole face in that shit, I wasn't afraid to get my face wet. I licked and slurped like I was trying to get to the center of a tootsie pop. I circled my tongue around on her clit. The next thing I knew she started squirting and I opened my mouth to catch all of it. I was introducing her to various pleasurable moments, but there were more things I would make her body do.

I came up from between her legs and placed my full lips on hers sticking my tongue in her mouth. I eased out of my briefs being sure not to break our kiss. My eight-inch-wide curve chocolate dick, full of thick veins was standing at attention. I placed the head at her entrance just rubbing it against her wetness. I eased the head in slow and easy, and her body tensed up immediately. I was having the damnest time getting the head in alone. I eased it in inch by inch, and the fit was tight as hell when I finally got the whole thing in. A nigga didn't know how to act with some untouched pussy.

This was one of the reasons I said she was delicate, and I would handle her with care. She was mine, and I was getting ready to mark my territory. I knew that she was hurting by my size from her moans and the look on her face but if she just gives it a little time she would feel more pleasure than pain. I would make sure of that, tonight was all about her. This was her first time, and it would be a memorable moment for her. I wanted to be something she could always look back on, and her juices start to flow just knowing what I did to her on this specific night.

I grinded in and out of her trying to open her up with ease. I could feel her wetness surrounding my dick like I was skinny dipping in an ocean. Her tightness had a mean grip on my dick, it was like something I never experienced before. It was like her pussy was lock and my dick was the key, the two were made for one another. One would be useless without the other, the perfect match. Shit, she was my missing puzzle piece.

Her moans turned from pain to gratification quickly. I sped my pace up with every moan that escaped her lips. By now she was underneath me, and we were grinding to our own beat, but we were in synch with one another. Her manicured stiletto nails were scratching up my back, but I didn't give a fuck, it turned me on even more. Let me know I was tearing that shit up, I was going to put a hurting on this pussy to let her know what the fuck Khalil was about. I was giving it to her like this to let her know that I was hers and nothing or no one would deter me from her, and vice versa because I would be damned if I let her get away.

I asked her to turn over and toot it up. She did as she was told and I instructed her how to put an arch in her back. I didn't mind teaching her, this was a learning moment for the both of us. As I sexed her, I paid close attention to every moan, look of pleasure, and grunt to know what pleased her and what didn't. I was just that observant with my woman. I eased back in and picked up the pace as I pulled her into me by her waist. To keep from moaning loudly, she bit into the pillow. At this moment I wasn't showing any mercy as I choked her from behind. Not hard enough to cut off her breathing but enough for her to feel where I was coming from. It was all out of pleasure.

We were fucking like rabbits, and I was surprised as hell to see her throwing it back. I loved it though, her plump brown ass was slapping against my pelvis making clapping noises like it was a revival at a black Baptist church. Her wetness sounded like someone was stirring a bowl of pasta salad, shit had a nigga's mind gone. Not being able to hold it in any longer I pulled out and busted all over her ass. I got up and went into the bathroom for two warm rags. I wiped my nut off of her and asked her to lay down, so I could clean her up before cleaning myself. Once we both were clean, we just laid down pillow talking in one another's arms.

Today I found the true Bonnie to my Clyde. Like Neyo said 'I'm a movement by myself, but I'm a force when we're together'.

From this day forward, we would be untouchable.

Chapter 6

KEHLANI

I woke up with a smile on my face as I remembered the night Khalil and I just experienced. I didn't plan on losing my virginity last night, but I didn't have one regret. Last night he made me a woman. He made my body do things I never knew it was capable of doing. I was happy to give it to him because I knew that he would know just what to do with it.

It was evident that Khalil had strong feelings for me. With every moment that we spend together, I could feel my feelings for him getting stronger and stronger. The way that he cared for me was unlike anything I've ever experienced before.

All of the other guys that have crossed my path only had one agenda in mind, and that was to get between my legs. When they realized that they weren't getting anything more than conversation They went for the females that they knew were putting out. That was cool though because I was waiting until I was ready.

See with Khalil it was different, and I knew that everything he did for me was out of the kindness of his heart. He wasn't looking for anything in return. He never pushed up on me in a sexual way, we've never even talked about sex. We could be in each other's presence without any type of sexual activity being involved. We just genuinely enjoyed one another's company.

The way he came to my rescue when he heard what Fred was trying to do to me made me feel butterflies all over. The way that he was about to take a life for me let me know that he loves me. You don't go to those extreme measures just for anybody. I pulled the trigger myself out of anger, but if I hadn't, there was no doubt in my mind that he would have. That'll forever be embedded in my mind.

After school, I had plans on going home to check Aretha to see if she noticed anything suspicious. I could just imagine what type of bullshit she had waiting for me once I got home. I would worry about that then because I had a good mind to let her ass know that I was leaving for good. When I turn eighteen, I would come back for JJ and get full custody of him.

Khalil was getting ready for work and JJ, and I was getting ready for school. I was just praying that today would be smooth sailing. After the three of us were done getting ready we left the house. We stopped at Hardee's for a quick bite to eat.

Khalil pulled up to the school to drop us off. He walked around to the passenger side to open the door for me. He pulled me in for a tight hug and planted a soft wet kiss on my lips. I hated to leave his side, but my education was a must. If I don't do anything else, I was going to get that advanced diploma.

I walked into the schoolhouse with a Kool-aid smile on my face. I haven't talked to Autumn since I asked her to leave my house that day. I was over her little jealous spell, and I prayed that she was also. She was standing at her locker grabbing her books for class. I walked up behind her and covered her eyes with my hand.

"Guess who?"

"I know it's you, Lani, I would know the scent of your perfume from anywhere."

She turned around and hugged me, and I returned it. That led me to assume that our little beef was squashed just like that. We began to walk to our homeroom class, greeting a couple of classmates along the way.

"You got a little glow going Autumn, let me find out that you have a little boo or something you didn't tell your bestie about," I said.

"Nah girl, it's nothing like that. I'm just in a good mood that's all."

"Hmph. Okay then."

The day went by quicker than I expected it to. Khalil shot me a text to let me know that he was parked outside waiting for JJ and me. I offered Autumn a ride home, but she said that she had a way. Khalil greeted me on the passenger side of the car as always to kiss me and to open the door for me like the true gentleman that he was. Now I was dreading going home to see Aretha's face, but I knew that eventually, I would have to face the music. JJ would be right there with me, we would face everything together.

After kissing my honey goodbye, I proceeded to walk in the house with JJ following closely behind. When we walked into the house the first thing I noticed was empty liquor bottles sprawled all over the coffee table. I immediately started thinking *"what the fuck?"* We just walked in like we normally would.

"It's nice to see y'all two since y'all don't know where the fuck home is," she spat as she blew cigarette smoke into the air.

Not wanting to get into it with her we both just pretended not to hear her. She was sloppy drunk and slurring her words. This shit was strange as hell because I've never known her to be a heavy drinker since I've been living under her roof. She just looked pathetic. It was only two days later since everything happened with Fred, so she couldn't have known about that. Just as I was thinking that the news started blaring loud as hell on the TV.

"A missing 68- year old Montgomery man by the name of Fred Jones has been missing for a couple of days. If anyone has any information on his whereabouts, contact the Montgomery Police Department," the news reporter stated.

Aretha bawled out so loud, now I knew why she was crying. Because Fred was "supposedly missing". That nigga could rot in hell for all I gave a fuck. If I had to do it all over again, I would without a second thought. If she knew what that man tried to do to me, she wouldn't really care about his whereabouts. Then again, she probably wouldn't give a fuck. It isn't like she ever held a care for us. She was only in it for the money, if they weren't cutting her ass a check every month, we would still be orphans.

She just sat there and cried all day like she had lost her best friend. Hell, they weren't even together that long, I wasn't even sure if they were even in a relationship. She was more concerned about him than where we had been these last couple of days. I had enough of this scene for the day.

"I'm leaving," I said to Aretha.

"And just where the fuck do you think you're going? Nowhere because nobody wants you...neither one of your good for nothing asses. If it wasn't for me the both of you would be in foster care."

"Bitch fuck you! You never did a mutherfucking thing for me or my brother. All your old ass wants to do is sit back and collect those damn checks every month. You're an old tired ass bitch who don't have shit to live for. I hope your ass rot in hell right alongside Fred," I spat mad as hell.

She had me all the way fucked up, I had taken enough of her bullshit, and I no longer gave a fuck. I was talking to her ass like she wasn't damn near fifty years, my senior. I wouldn't give a fuck if she was Harriet Tubman herself and she got wrong with me, I would buck on her ass too. You had to give respect to get it, some people felt like just because they were your elder, you had to respect them but nah, fuck that!

Her words stung like I just was stung by a yellow jacket. To hear someone say such hurtful things to me hurt me to my core. If she was going to treat us the way she did she could have just left us in foster care. At least there we didn't have all this animosity every day. She made it impossible to have a good day living with her unless she was at work. When she worked doubles my days went by pleasant as hell, but now all of that was dead. Other than providing somewhere for JJ and me to lay our heads, she didn't do a damn thing for us. I was leaving this bitch, and I wasn't looking back. Hate was such a strong word, but I didn't feel nothing but hatred towards her. If that bitch was on fire in front of me, I wouldn't throw an ice cube at her ass. That's just the way she made me feel towards her.

"Let's just go Lani," JJ said.

That was the best thing for me to do. I went into my room and grabbed all of the things that were valuable to me and JJ did the same. I knew that if I had to stay in that house a second longer, I was going to slap the shit out of her with no remorse. We left her house walking, my pressure being up from still being angry. I called Khalil to come scoop us up, we waited for him at Autumn's house. I was so angry; my leg was moving a mile a minute as tears steadily rolled down my face. My best friend was there to console me, and I appreciated her for that. If no one knew firsthand what

JJ and I went through with Aretha, it was her. I was done with her ass, and soon karma would hit her ass.

Shortly Khalil pulled up and got out of the car once he saw the expression on my face. He pulled me in for a tight hug, and I just laid my head on his chest and let the tears fall freely. He wiped them away and when our eyes met, and he told me that everything was going to be okay and that he got me. Suddenly everything was alright. I got into the car while he and JJ put our bags in the trunk and we pulled off once they were done.

I guess Aretha was too drunk to mention the 'break-in' or the fact that I said I wished she'd rot in hell alongside Fred, but I couldn't worry about that shit right now. We went through Burger King's drive-thru to get a quick bite to eat since I wasn't in the mood to cook anything. We sat around in the living room and watching TV.

"Bae, I have to step out for a minute. It'll be a little while so don't wait up for me," he said kissing me on my cheeks.

I was so drained I couldn't even question him

about where he was going so late. I took my bath, said my prayers, and went to sleep.

Chapter 1

KHALIL

I had a hit to do tonight, but I couldn't tell Lani that. Now wasn't the time for me to reveal my truth to her. My hit was a nigga named Boss. He was a flashy ass nigga that liked to showcase everything he had. He let it be known that he was getting money. Every time you saw the nigga, he was draped up in diamonds and in a nice ass fit. Whenever he hit the club scene him, and his people were in VIP throwing money around like it grew on trees or some shit. I had paper for days, but a motherfucker didn't know what kind of money I was sitting on because I didn't flaunt it. That just wasn't my style, I preferred to keep my shit lowkey.

See niggas like him made my job easier. They were easy targets and was never too hard to find. It was the first Tuesday of the month, so I knew that Club Envi was bound to do numbers, so I knew that nigga Boss would be in attendance. I was in an unmarked '99 black box Chevy with limo-tinted windows. I was dressed in black jogging pants with a black hoodie, with my all black timbs on my feet. I had my seat reclined all the way back, so I could go unnoticed. I sat in the back of the parking lot ducked off where there wasn't too much light shining.

Hassan had a hit out on Boss's head because he felt that he didn't pay his debt. Hassan fronted him some dope, and he has yet to bring back the profit. Yet, he was club-hopping every week, popping bottles and shit. Unappreciative of what the nigga did for him, the way he looked out not too many people do that anymore. He had been avoiding him for weeks, and now Hassan has grown tired of him giving him the run around about his money. He has been gracious as hell with the payback period and now his time has expired.

I grabbed my pre-rolled blunt from behind my ear. I placed the blunt between my lips as I watched the door of the club intently as a few people started to leave, mainly females. I struck fire from my lighter as I put the lighter to the end of the blunt. Inhaling a couple of times to get it burning how I wanted, then I exhaled. This purple haze had me feeling at ease, and I was in my zone. It was almost three o clock now, so I knew that the club was shutting down. I sat in my car for hours, but I knew that nigga was in there. He wouldn't miss this shit for the world, this was always his type of scene.

Just as I expected, after everyone had thinned out and the parking lot was practically empty, he came stumbling out with two bitches on his arms who I assumed were strippers. One had a low brush cut that was dyed blonde, and the other had on a burgundy wig. Their bodies weren't hitting on shit, but I guess this nigga didn't have a preference. I continued to watch them as I smoked my blunt. The nigga was fucked up, I could tell by the way he was using both women for support to stand up. If it wasn't for them standing there, he would be on the ground by now. Silly ass nigga.

They entered his 2017 Cadillac CTS. The woman with the blonde bald head got in on the driver side after the both of them helped him into the front seat. The other woman entered the back of the car, and they drove off right after she was settled. I pulled off right after them being sure to keep three car lengths behind them. They drove for a good little while, and now we were in the country. I followed behind them slowly as they entered a country back road. They were oblivious to the fact that I was following them because I turned my lights off. They parked in the driveway of a double-wide mobile home. It was nice as hell, cream-colored with baby blue shuttles. This nigga had a nice ass spot on the outskirts of the city but didn't want to pay up. I couldn't do anything but shake my head because he was on some low shit.

They exited the car with the both of them holding him up as he went up the stairs. I sat in my car for about twenty minutes as I gave them time to get settled in. I put my ski mask on my face, my gloves on my hands, and made sure my Glock was locked and loaded before exiting the car. I tightened my hood on my head as I inched towards the house. I could see the light from the living room peeping through the door. I walked soft as hell on the stairs leading to the front door, and I saw that the door wasn't closed all the way. They were making it easier and easier for me. I opened the door slowly being careful not to make any noises. There was no one in the room, but I could hear moaning and laughter from the back of the house. I creeped through with my gun leading the way, tip toeing all the way down the hall.

I put my silencer on as I got closer to the room they were in. I peeped through the crack of the door, and the nigga was laying down getting his dick sucked while the other female rode his face. I was sure that they were only in it for the money because Boss was not an attractive nigga at all. The nigga face looked like he'd been through many trials and tribulations. Yet, he had hoes falling at his feet because he had a little dough. That's all these hoes wanted. When I think on it they probably were trying to set his ass up as well by the way they left the door open and shit. That meant I need to do what I came to do and haul ass before the next nigga come to do the job.

The bald head one was going to work on his ugly ass as her head bobbed up and down. They were all into what they were doing that they were oblivious to me standing in the doorway. Their eyes were either rolled to the back of their head or closed. I sent a silent shot to the back of the blonde bitch's head killing her instantly, making her fall on his stomach.

"Why'd you stop? That shit was feeling heavenly," he said with his eyes closed. When he finally opened them, he saw me, and I knew he could've shitted bricks. He had no clue who I was, but I was sure that he knew what I was there to do.

"Oh, shit man wtf."

"Oh, shit is right my nigga!" I said and sent one shot hitting him in the head, and blood started oozing from it. Ol' girl started crying hysterically, and I put her out of her misery with the quickness. I don't have time to hear her beg and plead for her life. It was nothing personal to either women, they were just casualties, and I never left a witness behind. I tucked my gun in the back of my pants before I looked for some dough to get because I know the nigga had it. I opened up his closet, and he had two duffle bags full of stacks tucked in the wall. It wasn't hard to find at all. I grabbed them and wiped down the doorknobs before leaving. Even though I had on gloves, there was nothing wrong with being extra careful.

I got into the car and threw the two duffle bags on the floorboard on the passenger side. I left out of the driveway with my lights off until I was out of dodge and felt it was safe to turn them back on. I called my boy Terrio to let him know I was swinging through the chop shop for him to get rid of this car. When I got there, I gave him 10 stacks just for him always looking out with the cars when I needed them. I fucked with him the long way, and I knew he had a family to feed, so ten stacks wasn't shit. He dropped me off a block away from my car, and I walked the rest of the way.

When I made it to my car, I headed over to Hassan's. I walked in with both duffle bags as I entered into his study.

"I got a little some from the hit, it was three birds with one stone situation. You feel me?" I said talking in code to let him know two other people was murked alongside with him.

"I trust that you did what you had to do."

I opened up the duffle bags to show him the content.

"This should make up for what he owed you."

"You know what you keep that Youngblood. Your loyalty to me and your work ethic is the reason why I fuck with you the way that I do. What you just did most niggas wouldn't even have thought about doing, and I respect that."

"And vice versa my nigga, I appreciate you."

We chopped it up for a little while longer, and I headed home to be under my woman. All the way there all I could think about was her. It's crazy as hell that I was the ruthless nigga I was, killing being my occupation but when it came down to Lani I was soft as cotton. She held a special place in my heart, and I would cherish her indefinitely. I wouldn't necessarily say that I felt guilty about her not knowing what I did to live the way that I do. I wasn't proud of what I did, but I wasn't ashamed either. It was something that just kind of happened and I've been in this life ever since.

Hassan has looked out for me and has had my back since I was a jit. In a way, this was my way of repaying him by staying in the business as his hitman. He needed me just as I needed him. He helped me to live comfortably, and in return, I eliminated his enemies, whoever they may be. By no means did I want to come off as a nigga who liked to keep things from my woman. I just had to find a way to break it to her gently. When the time was right, I would explain everything to her. I didn't want anything to disturb the peace that we had in our relationship right now. If anything, I wanted to be the one to bring her peace because lord knows she has endured enough pain.

When I made it home, the house was quiet as hell, so I knew that Lani and JJ were asleep. I got out of the clothes I just had on and took a quick shower. Once I was finished I snuggled up next to my bae, I pulled her close to me as we spooned. I laid there for about an hour just thinking on shit. I eventually fell into a deep slumber. I woke up when I felt Lani stirring around in her sleep. She was mumbling and crying, begging someone to stop. By her cries, I knew exactly what she was dreaming about. I shook her until she was awake, and she still was crying. All I could do was hold her and let her know that I was there for her. If I could bring the nigga back alive to kill him all over again, I would. He really deserved to die a slow death.

No words were spoken as I sat in the bed with my back against the headboard and Lani in my arms. I kissed her softly on her forehead. I knew that today was a rough day for her, so I wasn't going to pressure her into going to school today. There was no need for her to go and not be able to focus in class. I knew that it wasn't as easy to shake that thought away. She caught her first body. Even if she thought that it wouldn't phase her because it didn't when she pulled the trigger. I knew that eventually, it would I've been in her shoes before. With time all wounds heal, I knew that to be a proven fact.

I got up for a hot minute just to let JJ know that he didn't have to go to school either if he didn't feel up to it. He said that he would stay in to try to get some proper rest. He too had tossed and turned all night.

Lani's 18th birthday was a month away so I was brainstorming on what to do to make her special day everything she wanted it to be and more. Maybe another trip out of the state. She seemed to enjoy our time in Florida, I would make it my business to ensure that she wears a smile on her face the whole day.

She was sleeping so peacefully in my arms. I decided then and there that today would be the day that I come clean with her. Our relationship was fairly new, but we've already experienced a lot of crazy shit together. She probably couldn't even see me as that type of nigga, but I am who I am. I never pretended to be anyone else. I just laid there holding her as I thought about how I would tell her exactly. Fuck it, I just have to spit it out, no need to sugarcoat it. I just stared at her, admiring her beauty. Her beauty was breathtaking, her skin was so pretty and smooth. I loved the way her eyebrows were naturally full and her lips also. Makeup was solely an option for her because she was still beautiful as hell without it. Her natural hair complimented her beauty as well.

She must have felt me staring at her because she woke up and looked directly into my eyes. I gave her a half smile, and she immediately asked me what was wrong. Just by the look on my face, she could tell that something was bothering me.

"I need to talk to you about something serious.

This is hard as hell for me to say to you, but I want to be open and honest with you."

"Okay Khalil…you're scaring me."

"I don't mean to scare you bae." I swallowed the big lump in my throat. I never said the words out loud, and the only person that knew what I did was Hassan.

"When I reveal my truth to you I hope that it doesn't change anything between us. I want to be with you, but if what I'm about to tell you deters you away from me, I can't do anything but accept it. I never lied to you about working for Foot Locker, but you know that doesn't pay for all of this fancy shit I have."

"Do you sell drugs?" she asked me.

"Nah ma, just let me finish…I murk niggas for a living. I'm a hired hitman, I kill niggas for a living, and I feel nothing when I do it. I'm not proud of it, but this is the only life I've ever known. I've been on my own since the age of fourteen. I met a cat that took me under his wing and gave me work to keep me from living on the streets. This has been my only means of survival for as long as I can remember. When I say this is all I know, this is all I know Lani. I wouldn't ever let my work come in between us or our relationship. But if you want to walk away from this, I have no choice but to respect your decision."

She said nothing for a couple of minutes, but it felt like a couple of hours. I didn't know what else to say. I was waiting for her to give me a response. The silence was killing me, and it made me anxious to know what she would decide. At the same time, I was afraid that I might lose her.

"Khalil I can't judge you... hell, I'm no saint myself. I can't judge you for what you've been through in your past. You did what you had to do with the cards you were dealt. I don't feel no different about you, my feelings are the same. I'm not going anywhere so you can erase that thought from your mind, you're stuck with me," she said smiling. I kissed her immediately as the feeling of love took over me.

I never had someone who was willing to stick with me through whatever. Hell, my parents didn't have me the way she does, that was evident in the way they just gave me up as a child. Me telling her that I was a hitta was something that I expected her to run away from, but she ensured me that she wouldn't. She understood me on a level that no one else ever had. I knew that she was my rider.

"I love you." I said looking deep into her eyes.

"Promise to never leave me."

"I Love you more Khalil, and I promise to never leave; as long as you continue to keep a smile on my face."

"You got that gorgeous." We made passionate love the entire day.

Chapter 8

AUTUMN

I sat in the bed with my bra and shorts on as Deon bagged up his weed. I was scrolling on FaceBook laughing at memes.

"Chill with all that laughing shit, I'm trying to concentrate."

"I'm sorry babe", I said as I put my phone down. I got up from the bed and walked over to where he was sitting at the table. I walked up behind him placing both of my hands on his shoulders and started massaging them, and then ran my hands down his bare chest. I pushed the table back to allow myself access to the front of his body. I walked in front of him and placed one of my legs onto his and then the other straddling him. He held on to me so that I wouldn't fall. I tried to kiss him on his lips, but he turned his head, so I started kissing and sucking on his neck instead. He wasn't about to fuck up my mood by not kissing me. I had one agenda in mind, and that was to get my rocks off.

Normally he wouldn't let me do anything but suck him up, but right now I felt I had him just where I wanted him. I wasn't an ugly bitch by a long shot. A little darker than most but you know what they say, "the blacker the berry, the sweeter the juice." I was slim thick with my curves in all of the right places, but yet I couldn't compare to Kehlani. I can't front; she was a beautiful girl. Tonight, I was determined to make him forget that bitch ever existed. I know y'all probably wondering how I could talk about my "bestie" that way. But y'all can't judge me; she was a bitch in ever since of the word.

The truth is I've always been jealous of her. For the life of me I couldn't seem to understand how a person who was dealt the cards she was, still got everything she wanted. It was plenty of times we went places together and would meet guys and the best-looking one always wanted her. I just got the scraps with the ugly friend. No matter how revealing my clothes were, I still was overlooked. Imagine that shit. Don't get me wrong, I love my friend. She was really the only true friend I ever had. Over the years I've just grown tired of her getting it all, I wanted to win for once. Granted this wasn't supposed to be a competition, but at times that's exactly what it would feel like.

I knew that me fucking with Deon was low as hell, but what she didn't know wouldn't hurt her. It gave me a rush to be creeping behind her back. Deon wasn't innocent in any of this either. We were grown enough to know what we were doing was wrong, but we still didn't stop. It wasn't like she really wanted him anyways. I knew firsthand how he was just her money man. I never felt that she really cared for him that way. She chose Khalil, so that's who she gets. I focused my attention back on Deon when he started tugging at my shorts. I stood up and went ahead and took my shorts off without his help. I was wearing a thong underneath. I straddled him again with the thong still on. He unhooked my bra, and my tits popped up, happy to be free from the bra. My nipples were standing at attention, daring him to show them some attention. They were big as hell and pointy, he immediately took one in his mouth, squeezing the hell out of my tit in the process.

Temperatures were definitely rising, and at this point, I knew that he couldn't refuse me if he wanted to. I had him eating out of the palm of my hands. I started kissing and sucking on his tattoos on his neck, and it drove him wild. Not being able to contain the excitement I slid my thong to the side and placed his dick at my gushy entrance. He didn't budge so I took that as my opportunity and a sneaky grin spread across my face. Bingo! I lifted my body up enough so that I could ease down on it nice and slow. He let out a light manly moan. I sat all the way down on it until it disappeared inside of me. I began to gyrate my hips back and forth at a nice steady pace. Deon grabbed me by my waist tightly and started making me bounce up and down on it. I was moving my hips and twerking like I was in a Ying Yang Twins video. He tapped me on the ass indicating for me to get up and I lifted up off him and stood up. He pushed me in my back and made me arch my back. He entered me without warning and immediately started beating it up. It was painful as hell at first but soon after I caught his drift, I started throwing it back like my life was depending on it. This wasn't any lovemaking we were straight fucking, but I was loving this shit.

In my mind, I knew that once he got a taste of this good shit, he wouldn't want anything else. Also, it would be hard as hell for him to stop fuckin with me now. I knew exactly what I was doing. I tightened my pussy walls every time he slid in and out. The nigga didn't know what to do! I had him. I could've sworn I heard him call me Lani, but I disregarded and kept doing what I was doing. It wasn't long after that I felt him shoot all of his kids up inside of me and I came simultaneously. He was being really reckless with that shit, but I just took it as he no longer gave a fuck. Hell, it is what it is.

Once we were finished, I went into the bathroom to clean myself up. I went to lay down on the bed and Deon broke my ass up really quick when he told me to get dressed, he had some moves to make. I guess he wasn't into the cuddling after sex shit, but I wasn't tripping at all. I finally got what I have neem wanting, and I was happy as hell about it. I got dressed and went outside to wait on him to come out to take me home. When I pulled up to the house Shaunie, and my mother was sitting on the porch. I rolled my eyes in my head because I knew they were coming with the twenty-one questions. He stopped the car, I grabbed my bag out the backseat and made my way up the stairs leading to the porch.

"Mmmm.. miss thang! What is Deon doing dropping you off?" Shaunie asked.

"Mind your business Shaunie."

"Isn't that the same guy that rides through here looking for Lani?" my mama asked looking at Shaunie.

"Yeah ma, that's him," Shaunie answered.

"I hope you know what you are doing little girl, wanting to be grown before time is going to catch up to your ass!" She said to me, and I just walked into the house rolling my eyes, and slamming the screen door in the process.

I had no time for what they were talking about.

They didn't know what was up with us and even if they did, they couldn't judge me or the situation I had. I wasn't ashamed of anything I was doing, and they wouldn't make me start feeling guilty. Not today or any day, I wouldn't let them. I was practically grown now and any decisions I made I would be the only one who would have to reap the repercussions from it. I know my mama was referring to me fooling around behind my best friend back, but I wasn't about to stop. We have crossed the lines, and now it was too late to turn back. This was a dangerous game we were playing, and I knew that. I would continue to play my role as the secret bitch.

I was sure that Deon still possessed feelings for Lani, but he couldn't have her if he wanted to. She was now Khalil's woman officially, and Deon was just a thing of the past. So, he might as well suck that shit up and accept what he has in me. In the end, I was the only one in his corner as of now.

I had been home for a little over three hours, and I was bored out of my mind. Deon wasn't texting me back or answering my phone calls. I figured he was still out in the streets handling his business. When he wanted to fuck with me, he would hit my line, and I would be there waiting. I decided to call Lani to see what she was doing since I had nothing else to do. She told me that she was at the house chilling and asked if I wanted to have a little girls date at the house and I agreed. I was getting ready to walk down the road to her house when she told me that she wasn't there and that she would be through to come get me. That threw me for a loop, but I didn't say anything. I got dressed and grabbed my PJ's for our movies date as I waited for her to pull up. About fifteen minutes later I heard a horn blow outside, and I knew it was her. I walked through the living room, and I could feel my mama rolling her eyes at me as I walked by. She was judging the fuck out of me.

"If you think the little slick shit you doing won't catch up to your ass you have another mutherfucking thing coming. You have some devilish ass ways just like your two-timing ass daddy," she hissed at me before taking a pull from her Newport.

I just ignored her bitter ass, fuck what she was

talking about! I would continue to do me, I don't give a fuck how anyone felt about it either. I didn't see Shaunie, so I guess she left the house while I was in my room. When I walked outside, I saw Khalil's Charger out there, and I rolled my eyes in my head. She was pushing his nice ass whip. I see now that this relationship was closer than I thought. I got in and hugged her as we pulled off. We arrived at a house who I assumed was Khalil's. By the way, Lani was so comfortable with everything I could tell that she was used to this environment. When we walked in JJ was sitting in the living room playing the game like he was at home. I was thinking to myself *"was this home for them?"* The shit was weird as hell. The more I thought about it, I haven't seen either of them in the hood in a while. But then again, I was creeping around with Deon, so I couldn't keep up with what they had going on. I was too busy trying to keep my shit under wraps.

"Supp JJ."

"What's hannin Autumn? I'll be out of y'all way in just a second."

"Same ol same, and you good take your time.

I'm the guest here." I said with a sarcastic laugh.

"Girl cut the shit," Lani said laughing.

JJ wrapped up his game and Lani went into the back to change into her pajamas. She showed me to the bathroom, and I changed into my pajamas as well. When I finished getting myself together, she had everything set up in the living room. She had everything down to the microwaved popcorn, hot cocoa, and all of our all-time favorite movies. It was a girl's day, and I honestly thought it would be a good time. We decided to watch Friday, you could never go wrong with that one. We popped the movie into the blu-ray player and sat on the floor and ate popcorn and drunk juice. We laughed and talked, and it honestly felt like the old days. For a quick second, I felt a tad bit of guiltiness, but I shook it off real fast. I would just enjoy this little moment we were having because I could tell that she was enjoying herself.

Oh well, I just pray that what's done in the dark didn't come to the light anytime soon.

Chapter 9

KEHLANI

I was enjoying the time that Autumn and I was spending together. She just didn't know how bad I needed this. Don't get me wrong I loved spending time with Khalil and my brother, but I missed being around my best friend. Other than at school we didn't hang out as much as we used to. I needed someone to talk to about all of these thoughts in my head, but I didn't feel like I could share certain things with her anymore. I could feel our relationship drifting away slowly but surely. Even though I still considered myself her best friend I just couldn't open up to her about the things that I have been dealing with lately. I was grateful to have Khalil and JJ by my side. I was having nightmares every other night, and it was starting to get the best of me. Just Khalil being there at night brought me comfort. That man was heaven sent, and I was grateful to have him in my life.

Shit with us has been happening fast but in no way did I want it to slow down. I was loving this rollercoaster ride we were on together. Our relationship was developing more every day, and I never thought I would find the type of love I have in him. It's like for every negative thing I had to endure he comes in and does something twice as great to make me happy. His everyday motive is to keep a smile on my face. It meant everything to me to have someone that genuinely cared about my wellbeing and happiness. The relationship that he and JJ has is heartwarming. He has become the big brother that he never had. He looks out for him the same way he looks out for me. That's how I know that what we have is real, the things he does for my brother he isn't obligated to, but he does it on the strength of him loving his sister. Khalil was a real man, one of the realest I've ever known.

Even after finding out what he did for a living my feelings for him were the same. He was still the man that saved me from gunfire at that party, saved me from being raped, and gave my brother and I a safe place to lay our heads and to be comfortable doing so. That alone showed me the type of heart he had. Sometimes we all have to do things in life that we don't want to just to get by. I knew that it was partially wrong but who was I to judge? I knew that he just wasn't out here murking niggas for nothing. The people he killed were bad people who did bad things. If that is all you've ever known, I can't expect him to give it up just like that. Some things are easier said than done and I believed this to be one. I knew niggas who killed for any damn thing. If a nigga looked at them wrong, being on the wrong side of town. Small, simple shit; niggas were killing over. Khalil wasn't out here on no reckless shit like that, he moved strategically.

I've been doing a lot of thinking myself, and it's been on my mind how I shot Fred with no remorse. Maybe I could do it for a living as well, right by Khalil's side. A Bonnie and Clyde type thing. I saw it as a way for me not to have to worry about him coming home or not at night. Instead, I knew that he would because I would be right by his side. I knew that it would take a lot of convincing, but I was going to work on breaking him down.

Of course, I would graduate High School first, so I would at least be able to say that I have my Diploma. I owed my parents that much, they would be proud to know that I finished school. I wouldn't dare let JJ in on this like we did that situation with Fred. He would be oblivious to the whole ordeal. I didn't want this life for him; I would keep him on the straight and narrow. I only have four more months of school left, and I would be crossing that stage to receive my diploma. That was an accomplishment in itself because not too many people make it this far. After all of the things that I've been through; from the death of my parents to more recent shit, people would expect me to fail. I wasn't going to though, I had a damn point to prove. No matter the curveballs that are thrown at you, you lift yourself up, wipe the dirt off, and make the best of every situation. Good or bad, make it yours.

I know that I can't just make it look like I'm just living off of Khalil once I graduate. I would have me a hustle that would be on the forefront. I don't know exactly what it would be, but it would be something legit that can show for the money that I would have. I wasn't a dumb broad, and as you see, I have the whole thing planned out. The only thing I have to figure out is what will be my cover-up job. Maybe Khalil could help me come up with something. Who knows, maybe we can start our own business together. I would bring it up to him tonight when he gets home because two heads were better than one and I was giving myself a headache as I tried to put so much together in my head at once. I feel in my heart that everything would work out how I want it to. Khalil will probably be against the idea in the beginning because he doesn't want anything to happen to me in this dangerous line of work. But I trusted that he wouldn't let anything happen to me, he has proven that on more than one occasion. Shit, as long as we had each other everything would be straight. I knew that there was a lot I needed to know in order to be as professional as Khalil, but I was more than willing to learn. Hell, before the night I shot Fred I never even fired a gun. No one would have never known that though because I wasn't afraid to buss it. I even had caught Khalil by surprise.

The nightmares that I been having were more so from Fred trying to rape me and not the actual shooting. Just the thought of him trying to be the first one to know what I felt like disgusted me and made me sick to my stomach. I don't regret that at all because he had it coming. He knew what he was doing was wrong, but that didn't stop him from trying to take advantage of me. He was a sick bastard and who knows if he tried that with any other young girl's before and succeeded. If so they wouldn't ever have to worry about him bothering them anymore. That old perverted bastard was gone and never coming back. Neither JJ or I heard anything from Aretha since she practically kicked us out of her house. The checks were still rolling so I was sure that was her main concern. She didn't know where we were, and I preferred to keep it that way. Khalil made sure we weren't wanting for shit, so she could keep that little ass piece of change she was getting once a month. Clearly, she needed it more than us.

It was starting to get late, and Autumn and I

have watched three movies and ate enough popcorn. I knew Khalil would be getting off work within the next hour, so I wanted him to be able to walk in a clean house when he got off. I dropped Autumn off and went back to the house to straighten up the living room to cook Khalil a quick meal before he arrived home. It was the least I could do for him taking care of us the way he did. I kept the house clean and intact and made sure he never went hungry. I already had some steak thawing in the sink so I all I had to do was clean it and then season it and cook it. I seasoned the steak to perfection and had it in the oven baking with assorted peppers and onions covering it. I sautéed some Roasted Parmesan Green Beans with butter and cut up some potatoes to make homemade mash potatoes. We would be having honey butter dinner rolls on the side and some Pinot Noir wine to wash the food down. I was moving fast as hell because I knew it wouldn't be long before he would be walking through the door. This was a quick an easy meal, and I knew that Khalil would love it just as he loves everything else I cooked.

I decided that I would bring up my proposition

to him over dinner. Hopefully, he doesn't say anything to get me upset because I've thought long and hard on this and I'm sure that this is what I want to pursue. I'd rather it be with him, but if he's not feeling it, I may feel obligated to make it happen for myself. Just as I was getting the steak out the oven, I heard Khalil come in.

"Damn bae, it smells good in here," he said as he walked up hugging me from behind and kissed me on my cheek.

"Thanks, bae, have a seat I'll fix your plate."

"Let me go wash up right quick, and I'll be back."

"Go ahead baby, do your thing."

I fixed our plates and waited for Khalil at the dinner table. I guess he decided to take a quick shower because it was taking him a little minute to return. I should have known that was what he was doing because that was the type of man he was. He liked to be clean, and I liked that about him. He wasn't one of those type of guys that believed that just because he was a man it was okay for him to be nasty. Khalil was far from that type, and that's why it was easy to live with him. I didn't have to clean up behind him and vice versa. When he returned to the din, he wore some grey gym shorts, a bare chest, as he used a towel to dry his curly hair. He walked in smiling at me, and those deep dimples made my heart melt. Bae was looking like an entrée right about now, and I wanted him instead of the food I just prepared. The man was looking good enough to eat. I knew that I had something important to talk about, so I wiped those freaky thoughts from my mind, momentarily. He sat down at the table, and we held hands and said grace together. That was one of the things that my parents instilled in me and JJ, and even up in age, it was something that I still preferred to do whenever I ate.

We made small talk as we ate, just catching one another up on our day. I was waiting for the right time to slip my proposition into the conversation. I can't lie. I was nervous as hell about it because I didn't want it to sound weird or crazy. I wanted him to take me seriously because I was serious as a heart attack.

Here goes nothing.

"Bae?"

"Supp bae," he asked as he placed a mouthful of green beans in his mouth.

"I have a proposition for you. I know that it's going to come off a little crazy but just try to keep an open mind as I speak.

"I'm listening Kehlani," he said as he wiped his mouth with a napkin.

I knew that I had his full attention now by the way he called me by my government name.

"Okay so...I've been doing a lot of thinking, and I want to be in on what you do. I want to help you carry out your hits, you know like your Bonnie or whatever."

"Really Lani, are you out of your mind? The shit isn't as simple as it may seem. You have to be trained for this shit. What makes you think you're built for the shit I do?"

"Khalil I can do it, just trust me on this. I'll finish school and everything, I'll even get a daytime job to make everything look legit."

"Lani I don't know about this, shit isn't sweet out here. I can't have you out here risking your life, for what? I take care of you for everything you need. I just can't see you out here on the shit I'm on man. I need you to focus on school and all that other shit. This isn't the life I want for you, I just don't know man. Just let me ponder on the shit for a while."

"That's fair enough."

I wasn't necessarily mad with his response because he didn't come right out and say no. So, there was a little ounce of hope somewhere in there, so I was cool for the night. I know that I'd just thrown a curveball at him, but all I wanted was for him to do as he said he would and sleep on it. JJ and I had school the next day, so I cleaned up what Khalil and I had and when JJ came home he ate. We went into our bedroom and prepared for bed. I knew that Khalil was tired because by the time I was done with my bath he was already sleep. I kind of wanted to get me some tonight, but at the same time, he needed to rest and have time to think on what I asked him. I cuddled up close to him, and instinctively he pulled me in closer and wrapped his arms around me. It made me feel warm inside, and my heart fluttered when he placed a soft kiss on the center of my back. Whenever he did that it just made me feel some type of way. In a strange way, it was like the kiss let me know that he loved me and cared for me. Strangely that's just how I saw the gesture. Either way, it made me feel good inside, and I went to sleep with a smile on my face and love in my heart.

***

She 'a pull the gun for me

Pop 2, she 'a take one for me

Set it off, if a bitch come for me

Set if off, if a nigga come for me

She 'a pull the gun for me

Pop 2, she 'a take one for me

Set it off, if a bitch come for me

Set it off, if a nigga come

Bryson Tiller's song "Set It Off," played on my beats speaker as I prepared for school. I've always loved this song but lately, I really been listening to the lyrics, and I feel it on a whole 'nother level now. I was for sure trying to be Khalil's ride or die; in more ways than one. I was already his companion, and now I was trying to be his partner in crime, only if he would have me. 'Set It Off' was our song in my eyes, it told our story in a way. I continued to get ready for school as I listened to the song on repeat and nodded my head to the beat. The song went hard as hell, and it was slept on just as Bryson Tiller was.

You been committed through this whole journey

Got a girl that don't expect as much from me

That's why she gets so much love from me

She just might be the one for me

Ain't no need to question, down bitch

That first verse always spoke volumes to me because it reminded me of what Khalil and I had. When we first met I didn't want anything from him but him. The fact that I wasn't out for anything, but his heart is the reason he did for me the way he did. It was never about what he could do for me or what I could get out of him. The situation was totally different than what

Deon and I had before. Don't get me wrong he always looked out when I needed him, but sometimes some things just can't be forced. He'll always be someone special to me, but I couldn't see myself having something serious with him. I don't know why, but I just couldn't. Khalil had me at hello, and I was just too stubborn to admit it. It caught me a little off guard because his boldness struck me, his sexiness intrigued me, and it turned me on at the same time. He knew what he wanted, and he stopped at nothing to show his interest in me.

I was all ready to go to school as I did the finishing touches on my natural hair. JJ and Khalil were in the kitchen eating a small breakfast waiting on me. I joined them at the table and ate my grits, eggs, and sausages that bae had prepared. Once we all were finished eating, we left the house and proceeded to the school. Khalil was off today, and I wish I could've spent the day with him, but I knew I would eventually. I'm just lucky to wake up to his face every day and fall asleep in his arms every night.

When we arrived at the school, JJ dapped Khalil

up and exited the car. I stayed seated just a little longer to say my goodbyes to him and of course, get my kiss. When I broke the embrace and looked towards the entrance of the school, I could have sworn I saw Deon's red Camaro, but I could have been tripping. There was no reason for him to be at the school. I don't even know the last time he and I spoke. It could've been anybody I told myself as I exited the car and proceeded to the entrance of the school. JJ waited for me at my locker, and he and I walked through the hallway together. I hadn't seen or heard from Autumn today, but I was sure she was at school. She rarely missed a day; school was her favorite pass time.

I went ahead and headed to my homeroom class, and she wasn't in there so shot her a text inquiring about her whereabouts. She never responded, but when the bell began to ring for first period, I saw her in the hallway.

"What's up girl? I texted you after I saw that you weren't in homeroom."

"Girl, I had to handle some shit, but I'm good now. What's up with you, you good?"

"Yeah, shit smooth my way, just ready to get this day over and done with."

"I second that motion," she said, and we laughed as we continued to class.

She never did say what she had to handle, and I wasn't the one to pry. If she wanted me to know I'm sure she would have told me. I just let it go and continued to try to make the best of the day. The day was going by swift as hell, and there were no complaints on my end. It was now around 12:30, and it was time for second lunch. I was a little late since I had to finish a test, so Autumn and a couple of our classmates were already seated once I entered the lunchroom. Proceeding to the lunch line, I was minding my business when I was sending Khalil a cute little text messages as I overheard two girls talking behind me.

"Yeah, that nigga Deon has been getting money for a while now. The things that I would do to his sexy chocolate ass and those slugs drive me crazy."

"Hell yeah, the nigga is fine as hell with that nice ass Camaro. He just fucks with all the wrong bitches. I saw that chick Autumn get out of the car with him this morning. I thought he fucked with her friend though, but we know these hoes never stick to the code anyway."

As I listened to them, talk I felt my face get hot and my blood instantly started to boil. It's like they were oblivious to the fact that I was the friend they were talking about or they just simply didn't give a fuck. Either way, the shit pissed me off, and it was taking everything in me not to say anything. These hoes as this school was so full of mess and drama and I was beyond ready to depart from this shit. I wouldn't have to worry about dealing with shit like this. I was far from the scary type; I just wasn't the one to indulge in bullshit, so I pretended not to hear them. I continued to fix my food and went to sit at the table with Autumn and everyone else. I continued texting Khalil as I played over my food. I can't lie all of the things they were saying kept replaying in my head. *Why would she be in the car with him,* I kept questioning myself. I knew they were cool when I was dealing with him, but from my understanding, their relationship was built off of the one he and I had. She was only around him when he was around me. The way that the girls tried to make it seem like they had something going on. Nah, I don't believe that. All I had to was ask her, but I didn't want to cause any unnecessary tension between my best friend and I. Shit with us has already been slipping. She was my best friend, damn near my only friend, and I didn't want to lose that bond due to some he say she say shit. It probably wasn't nothing but a harmless ride to school. At least that's what I made myself believe.

They were having a conversation of their own and to not make it so obvious that the wheels in my head were spinning. I began to participate in the conversation. One thing I knew though, if it was some fuck shit going on behind my back I would find out. What's done in the dark will always come to the light, and for now, I would act as if I was unmindful to it all.

Chapter 10

KHALIL

I had been doing some serious thinking about everything Lani said to me last night. Like I told her I would sleep on it and I did. I don't know why she wanted to do this, but it sounded like she already had her mind made up about it. Whether I agreed to let her do it or not, so I knew I had a choice to make. She had a point when she said that I wouldn't let anything happen to her and she was absolutely right about that.

   If I was to let her enter this field, there would have to be some training underway. This shit wasn't just for anybody, and I needed her to be on the up and up if she was going to be my partner. I never worked with anyone; all of my hits were carried out solo. I didn't need her slipping or fuckin me up anyway because I was accustomed to moving as a one-man army. That's just what I was used to but who knows, maybe she could be of some help to me and make shit go a little smoother in certain situations. I just dropped her and JJ off, so I was on my way to see Hassan to run the idea by him and see how he would feel about it. I hope he don't look at me like I had two heads, the way I looked at Lani when she said it to me. That shit caught me all the way off guard. Shawty was trill as fuck, and now her ass was trying to be a savage out here in these streets.

When I arrived at Hassan's crib, his lady told me that he was out back on the golf course, so I went around back to meet him. He was out there playing golf by hisself. One day I hoped to live just like him, retired doing what the fuck I want when I want. I just stood back waiting until he was done before I approached him. He saw me and told me to give him just a minute, and I nodded my head in agreeance. I went to take a seat on the patio in one of the lawn chairs as I waited for him to join me. As I waited for him to be done, I sat there and texted Lani. She was making me smile with all of these kissing emojis she was sending me. I think she was just really trying to butter me up though. She already knew she had me eating out of the palm of her hands. That was my baby girl, and she meant everything to me. Lani was my sunshine on a rainy day. I was blessed the day she walked into my life.

"What's up youngin? What woman got you smiling like that?"

"My girl Lani," I said laughing.

"She must be something special to have you cheesing like that. I never seen you this way, and I've known you for nine years."

"I know man and yeah she is very special to me. I never expected anyone to make me feel the way that she does. She brings out the best in me ya know? She is the reason that I'm here actually."

"What's on your mind?"

"Well, the thing is I'm in love with shorty, and I'm trying to be an honest person with her. It was becoming harder and harder having to leave her side at night and lying about where I was going. I didn't want her to think that I was out here fucking off of on her, so the only thing for me to do was tell her the truth. I told her what I did for a living, and I expected her to run away, but she didn't. The girl has my back like no one ever has, and I shocked myself the way that I'm so honest with her. I've never been like this with anyone. We had a little run in a little while back when her foster mother's boyfriend tried to rape her.

Just as I was about to murk the nigga, she came from behind me and pulled the trigger. Her brother and I got rid of the body, but shit was just crazy after that. Long story short they living with me now. Knowing what I do she wants to be in on the operation. I told her I would sleep on it and I did, but I just wanted your input on the whole thing being that I work for you."

"Do you think that she is capable to perform diligently in this line of work? This shit isn't for amateurs, and so far, we haven't had any hiccups when handling our business. You're capable of handling your business by yourself. It's really up to you if you want to go forward with this. I just hope that you know what you are doing. There is no room for emotions when doing this, and she's a female not saying a woman isn't capable, but you would know what your woman is capable of. She must be trained on shooting and a whole bunch of other shit just the way that you have. It would be something like a little trial and error, but what I will say is that you will be responsible for her and if anything should ever go wrong I'll be looking at you."

"I understand that, and I will make sure she gets all of the training and everything that she needs. We would start training immediately, but I won't allow her to actually start helping with the hits until she finishes school. That's a main priority and after that everything could get on the roll. I'm not going to let any mistakes happen. She would be trained to move the same way that I was. That's a promise, thank you for considering this. You won't regret it."

"Okay, please don't make me regret it. I'm doing this because out all of these years you've never have asked me for anything and you've always been loyal to me. I do expect to meet her, and I would play a part in her training just as I did with you. I would give her the same amount of respect that I give you. If you can bring her by tonight for dinner, and we will discuss things a little further."

"I can do that, I'll see you then," I said as I stood up and dapped him up.

I know that once Lani hears the good news she'll would be ecstatic but soon it'll be game time and I had to make sure that she knew what she was getting herself into. This shit was for real out here, and at any moment shit could go wrong. I wasn't expecting the worse but sometimes shit just happened that way. I still had a couple of hours before school would be out, so I went home to tidy up a little bit and to find something for us to wear to dinner.

I knew we should dress nice because knowing Hassan, this dinner would be elegant as hell. That's cool though because Lani, and I both cleaned up nice. The house wasn't nasty at all. I just wanted to straighten the pillows on the couch and put down some carpet freshener on the carpet and vacuum. I had my wax warmer burning in the living room with the berry cheesecake wax illuminating a nice aroma throughout the entire house. I went into our closet and decided on a burgundy button-down shirt with black slacks. I picked out a nice black dress for Lani. We wouldn't be too dressy, but nevertheless, we would be dressed nicely. I didn't want to do too much, but I still wanted her to leave an impression on Hassan and his wife. Her beauty was nothing that I had to worry about. In fact, when he sees her, it might just throw him off that she is the one that's trying to be a certified hitwoman.

Lani was a beautiful lady, and any man could see that. After I had everything picked out and laid out on the bed, I left home to head to the school. When I pulled up I saw JJ standing at a red Camaro talking to someone who I soon realized was the dude Deon that Lani used to kick it with. JJ started walking towards my car, and Deon pulled off headed in my direction. I just held a smirk on my face as Lani was approaching the car. I got out to greet my woman like I normally do, but this time I decided to put on a little show for his jealous ass. When she walked up, I went to hug her and squeezing her ass in the process.

I planted a sweet kiss on her neck, and her face met mine, and I kissed her with so much passion that anybody looking would be turned on, but I broke it before I got some shit started right there in the parking lot. I grabbed her bag from her and opened the door for her to enter. I placed the bag in the trunk before I pulled off from the parking lot. That nigga eyes were green with envy as he watched the whole fiasco. I don't know why I did that, maybe it was the little ounce of pettiness I possessed. Maybe it was because I knew that I had something he wanted so bad but will never be able to have. I knew that she was mine and she wasn't going anywhere. I bet that nigga tossed and turned every night at the thought of Lani being laid up with me. That was just my way of showing homeboy that he could let that little fantasy go. I had her, and I wasn't coming up off her, ever!

"What was that all about Khalil? That was a little extra don't you think?"

"Nah, I don't think it was extra at all, I just wanted homeboy to see who you belong to."

"Khalil as long as you and I both know what we have we don't have to prove shit to anyone. You got me, and you know that I'm not checking for anybody else. Not even Deon, okay?"

"Okay baby, I'm sorry about that. A nigga just got a little carried away."

"It's cool bae, just chill next time," she said, and her and JJ laughed.

I couldn't help but to laugh with them. I could admit that when it came down to Lani, she made every jealous bone in my body come out. Her assurance was all I ever needed though. I knew she was with me and I never had anything to worry about. She was a real one out here. I never had to question what she was doing when she wasn't in my presence because I knew what type of woman I had and vice versa. It was the same on my end, and that was something I was grateful for. We didn't have one of those relationships where not having trust in one another was a factor. Shit just went smooth with us. I guess you could say that we were equally yoked.

"JJ you want something to eat before we go home, or you'll just find something at home," I asked him.

"I'll fix me up something at home, we don't have

to spend any money on fast food."

"You sure?"

"Yeah, I'm straight bruh."

"Damn bae, you didn't ask me if I wanted anything,", Lani said sarcastically.

"I didn't ask you, babe, because we have somewhere we have to be tonight, and we'll eat there."

"Okay bae, that's cool."

I didn't want to tell her where we were going with JJ in the car with us. I wanted to keep everything involving that side of me at a minimum with him. He was a kid, and I didn't want him involved in anything else of that nature. He was innocent in all of this, and the less he knew, the better. We arrived home and just chilled until it was time for Lani, and I to get ready for our dinner with Hassan. She still had no clue where we were going yet. When JJ finished cooking his homemade burger and fries, he went into his room to play the game. I asked Lani to follow me into the bedroom.

Taking a seat on the bed, she had a seat beside me, and I began to tell her that I put some thought into what she asked me. I informed her that the dinner was for her to meet up with the boss man so that they could get acquainted and he could tell her what is expected from her.

"So, you're telling me that you agreed to let me do this with you."

"I guess you can say that, but as we stated before you will finish school and we'll have you trained accordingly. Are you sure this is what you want to do? Shit isn't sweet out here in these streets Lani?"

"I'm sure Khalil."

"Okay," was all I said as I kissed her on the lips and got up from the bed to get ready for the dinner.

We took a shower together as we took turns bathing one another and squeezing a quickie in; in the process. I dried her body off, and she dried mines off. We applied lotion to our skin and started getting dressed. As I buttoned up my shirt, I looked into the mirror as I noticed Lani putting her earrings in her ear. She looked stunning in her Glove Sleeve Skew Neck Black dress. She wore her natural hair; her makeup was soft with brown matte lipstick. This woman was fine, and I could feel my man rocking up all over again. If she wasn't careful, I would be trying to slide back in her one more time before we left the house. Damn! Her beauty alone had a nigga pre-cumming, and I couldn't control myself. My hormones were getting the best of me as I looked at her lustfully from behind. I checked my apple watch and noticed that I had at least, an hour to spare and that was more than enough time for me to do what I had to do.

She was now applying perfume to her wrists not paying any attention to me. Not wanting to get my clothes messed up. I took off my button-down now wearing my muscle shirt. I unzipped my pants and stepped out of them. I pulled my briefs down and let them fall to my ankles as I made my way to the nightstand where Lani was standing. I walked up behind her wrapping my hands around her waist, with her ass touching my mans.

"Khalil, what are you doing?" She asked me.

I turned her face towards to me and kissed her cutting off her words before she had a chance to speak again. I lifted up her dress until it was around her waist. I used my hands to caress her ass nice and gently as Ro James 'A.D.I.D.A.S' played in the background. Making this moment sexy as hell.

When your lips touched mine

It only confirmed what I already knew

I found true love in you

See one time I tried to love

I had my heart broken

I swore that I'd never love again see

But you changed my mind

All day I

Dream about sexing you (Oooh baby)

All day I

Dream about sexing you

I reached in front of her and entered two fingers inside of her, nice and gently. Pulling them in and out and twirling them around in a circular motion while they were still inside of her.

"Mmmmm," she moaned out so sexy.

As I was pleasuring her with my fingers, she reached down and started stroking my dick, and it was driving me crazy to see her silver glitter stiletto nails wrapped around my dick. I kept her nails done every two weeks because I found it so sexy to see her manicured hands wrapped around my dick. I started fingering her faster, and her body started to shake a little bit. I knew she was on the verge of cuming. I turned her around and picked her up and sat her on the dresser. She leaned her head back on the mirror, and I opened her legs and dived face first into her sweetness.

She tasted so good to me; I stuck my fingers back inside of her. When I took them out, both of them was filled with white cum. I put them both in my mouth and licked it all off and went back to sucking on her pearl. I sucked on her peach pearl like I was trying to suck the soul out of her. She held my head for dear life as she rode my face and soon her juices splashed all over my tongue. She was unable to utter a word as she continued to moan softly, trying to catch her breath.

Without warning, I got up from where I was and

entered her putting it all the way in, and she gasped. I was so far in that my dick disappeared, and I felt myself hitting the back of her pussy. One thing for sure was that she had walls and it was driving me crazy every time I hit that bih. It drove me crazier to know that I was the only nigga that ever had the privilege of experiencing this, experiencing her. I remember the night I took her virginity, she wanted me badly, but at the same time, I could tell that she was a little nervous. I believe any woman would be for their first time. I assured her that I wouldn't do anything to hurt her. I took it easy on her but still made it pleasurable for her. Now she was experiencing much more pleasure than pain, I broke her in, and she's no longer a rookie. Like Plies like to say, "she used to run from it, now she like pain." She was now a certified freak, almost as big of a freak that I am.

I was shoving my dick in and out of her forcefully. There was no love making right now, we were straight fucking, and I was on a mission to make her cum multiple times. I pulled out, and in one swift motion I placed her feet on the floor and bent her over on the dresser. I immediately started drilling her from behind, and the gushy sounds from between her legs were driving me insane. All you could hear was ass clapping and loud moans from her and groaning from me.

I was a man, but I didn't mind making noises during sex to let my woman know that she was satisfying me. I was loving this shit, and everyone knew raw sex was better. I wasn't fucking with nobody other than her and besides I get tested every month, and my bill of health was clean. I didn't just go around fucking off anyways. I pulled my dick all the way out until the point where it was nothing inside but the head.

"Pleaseeeeee Khalil put it back innnn."

"What's my name?"

"Khalilll."

"Nah what's my name?"

"Daddddddyyy."

"There you go," I said as I got a grip on her neck and stuck my dick back inside. I started beating it up sideways.

I could feel my nut building up, and I knew that I was on the brink of nutting. I kept the same pace as I had before.

"Come with me Lani," I said in sexual manly tone.

"I'm cumiiiinnngggg," she said, and I followed suit.

I collapsed on her back, and we laid there for about thirty seconds. That there was one for the books. I went into the bathroom to grab both of us warm rags. I laid her down on the bed and cleaned her up before doing myself. We freshened back up with our cologne and perfume, and we were out the door with big ass grins on our faces.

It wasn't nothing like a quickie before making a business run. *I could get use to this already,* I thought to myself. I had one hand on the steering wheel and another on her thigh. It didn't take long at all for us to make it over to Hassan's crib. As we pulled into the driveway, I saw the look of amazement on Lani's face. She was admiring the beautiful brick mansion that he lived in. The scenery of the neighborhood was just nice as hell anyway. One day I would have that, but right now I was stacking my money up until I had enough to live comfortably for a very long time.

"Are you nervous?" I asked her.

"I can't lie, I am babe."

"There is no need to be. Hassan and his wife are cool people. They'll make you feel right at home. Besides, I'll be by your side every step of the way."

"I know bae, that's why I love you."

"Love you too ma." I exited the car and went to her side to open the door for her.

"You beautiful ma, you know that?" I said as I walked behind her closely as we made our way to the door of the mansion.

"Thank you, daddy."

When we made it to the door I rang the bell, and someone came to answer. We waited in the foyer until Hassan's wife came to greet us. She complimented Kehlani on her beauty and style, and I knew that made her feel at ease. I was glad that they were hitting it off. I just wanted Lani to be as comfortable as possible right now. We were led to the dining area where a big table was already set. I pulled the chair out for Lani to have a seat and then Hassan's wife. We waited patiently for Hassan to join us; while we waited we sipped on some wine.

As we were making small talk, he made his entrance. He had a seat at the head of table and we said our introductions. I knew that this was a business meeting, but we would eat first before we got to discussing everything. His chefs prepared a five-star meal that was very pleasing to the taste buds. Now that dinner was out of the way it was now time to get down to the business.

Hassan questioned Kehlani as if she was in an interview, but technically I guess you could say that she was. I couldn't even tell that she was nervous anymore by the way she was handling her own. She answered everything he asked with ease and confidence. At that moment I knew just how serious she was about this. One thing that I knew about Hassan was that he liked for you to be on your shit at all times and always know what you're talking about. Lani was on point with everything.

The meeting was going smooth as hell, and I couldn't be happier. He told her that she had to be trained and she was willing to do whatever she needed to do. He saw something in her, and I knew that I was responsible for her. I didn't mind because she was my woman and her safety was my main priority. By the time she was done being trained she would be as skilled as I was.

Kehlani told Hassan that she would finish school first before getting into the business and I stood behind her on that. After we got what we came for we headed home, and my girl was in a great mood. I was happy to see her all jolly and smiling. The fact that he agreed to do this for Lani, and I showed me just how much he fucked with me, and I appreciated him for that. I guess we would be the modern-day Bonnie and Clyde or should I say Mr. & Mrs. Smith, either way, this would be a journey for the both of us. I still can't believe that this is what she wanted to do for a living.

We didn't need any unnecessary attention coming our way. See it was cool for me to have Foot Locker as my front but realistically, how would that job support me, her and JJ. She mentioned something to me about starting our own business, and it didn't necessarily sound like a bad idea. In fact, it was a great idea to show that we had a legitimate income coming in.

Lani was smart as hell, and she was good with her hands just as I was. We decided on a shirt shop, where we would make custom shirts and other items. I would leave it to Lani to come up with the name. I knew a cat that was in real-estate, and I would see about getting a small commercial building in the midtown area for starters. We had everything mapped out, and I think that the future was looking up for us.

I would be going into business with my woman and what better feeling could that be? We were about to get money together on all type of levels. Real power couple shit. Her birthday was only a week away, and I had a big surprise for her that I knew she would love.

Chapter 11

KEHLANI

My birthday was slowly approaching, and I was dying to know what kind of surprise Khalil had up his sleeves. He was so sneaky doing little things and making arrangements right under my nose. It wouldn't be long until I find out though. I tried to trick him into telling me what it was, but he won't budge. I would be turning eighteen and I would finally be legal. Not legal to the point where I can purchase alcohol, maybe in the hood stores but the only thing I could really buy was tobacco products. That was cool because I could now be able to go in the store and get my own blacks and not have to send anyone in there.

Some time had gone by since JJ and I moved out of Aretha's house. I grabbed a lot of my belongings, but we still had a lot of things there. We hadn't heard or seen her in a long time and strangely I had over ten voicemails when I woke up. When I started listening to them, it was her crying hysterically, and I knew instantly that she had been drinking. She was going on and on about how she knew that we killed Fred. I didn't give a fuck about what she was talking about because she didn't have enough proof to prove anything. For all, I was concerned she didn't have any proof. When I think about her I get sick to my stomach, she disgusts me as a human being.

How could she be the evil person she is and expect shit to just go right for her. That lady was sick in the head. She had us since we were young kids and were practically her 'children' and yet she didn't care for us the same way she did Fred. We been in her life much longer, but still, we meant nothing to her. I learned how to cope with it though, it doesn't bother me as much anymore because what I do know is that our real parents loved us unconditionally. I would forever hold that near and dear to my heart. Fuck Aretha!

I made it up in my mind that I would go see her today and get the rest of my belongings. I just hope that she doesn't be on no bullshit by the time I get there. I didn't have the time nor energy to go back and forth with her today. I just wasn't here for it. I was initially going to go by myself, but I thought against it and asked Khalil and JJ to go with me because I just had a gut feeling that some shit was going to go down. We sat around in the living room, and I let both of them listen to all ten of the voicemails that she left on my phone. I asked JJ did he hear anything from her, and he told me that he didn't.

That relieved me a little to know that she wasn't fucking with him, only me. She never really cared for me anyway, and the feeling was mutual. I tried my best to prepare myself mentally before leaving our house and headed to what used to be called my home. I had the two most important men in my life by my side, so that gave me the courage to go ahead. We left the house and proceeded to Aretha's crib.

As we turned on the street, I saw several bags on the front lawn, and I immediately lost it. I just knew that it was me and JJ's things. When Khalil parked, I hopped out the car so damn fast storming to the door. When I walked in, she was sitting down on the sofa in her robe with her legs crossed, rollers in her head like she didn't have one care in the world.

She had a Corona in one hand and a cigarette dangling from her lips. Her eyes held big black bags underneath like she hadn't slept in weeks. Knowing her, she probably didn't because all she could worry about was Fred's ass. The bitch had the nerve to put our shit out like it was trash or some shit. The nerve of this bitch! I had been playing shit cool and staying away from her, but she had a whole 'nother muthafucking thing coming if she thought that she was gonna play me on some hoe shit.

"What the fuck is up Aretha?! You are putting our shit on the fucking street like you giving shit away to the salvation army! What's your fucking problem, you miserable bitch?!"

"Little girl if you don't get the fuck out my house. I'm going to call the police!"

"Do what the fuck you have to do! As a matter of fact, let me give you a reason to call them," I said as I began to ransack her home.

I was angry as hell, and I was taking it out on the

house as I threw lamps and shit all over the place.

"Calm down Lani," Khalil said to me.

"Nah fuck that, this bitch got me fucked up! Hell, our money probably paid for half the shit in here. We never saw any of it, so this is my way of getting it back."

"Lani chill," JJ said, but I wasn't hearing any of that shit.

Everything they were saying was falling on deaf ears. I couldn't hear shit, it was like everything just was silent to me as I continued to do what I was doing. Aretha crying and throwing out accusations was what got me out of my zone.

"I know you had something to do with his disappearance you little sneaky bitch."

At this point, I had enough of this bitch, and there was nothing she could do to hurt me.

"That man tried to rape me, in your house! You are sitting up here crying about that mutheafucka who never even wanted you. The whole time the old bastard was plotting on ways to take my innocence for me. I hope that nigga burn slow he got just what he asked for. If you want I can send your ass right there to be with him."

I'm sure my words stung just like hers did so many times to me. I just didn't care anymore about this situation, Aretha, or Fred. After I said everything, I had to say the bitch hauled out and slapped me in my face. What the hell did she do that for because I was already a ticking time bomb? I punched her ass instantly creating a black ring around her entire eye. I didn't care she meant nothing to me just as much as I wasn't shit to her. She just laid-back crying holding her eye and I did her a favor and called the police myself.

I explained to them how my 'mother' was a drunk, and she was losing her mind, hallucinating, and making false accusations. I told them how she put me and my younger brother belongings out on the street for anyone to get them while we were visiting a friend. I went on and on, laying it on thick. She was fucking with the right one, and she would pay for it. The dispatcher informed that someone would be by there shortly and I just stood at the door huffing and puffing as my chest heaved up and down from being so pissed.

She was so lost in her zone that the bitch pulled out a little white bag from her robe and hit the bag right in front of Khalil, JJ, and me. This bitch was gone, but she was just making my little set up easier for me. She was unfit to be a mother and that right there was the proof. She had no clue that the police were on the way. The death of Fred turned her to drugs, and that was pathetic. Hell, for all I know she had been on the shit the whole time, she was just being discreet with it.

I saw blue lights creeping up the street, and I stood on the porch and waved my hand to let them know that I was the one who called. When the officer got out of the car, I gave him the same rundown that I gave the dispatcher, and he entered the house to see a high as a kite Aretha sitting on the couch looking deranged. I told him that I feared for her sanity and I just discovered today that she was on drugs all the while being a drunk.

He asked what happened to the house and I told him that she went crazy and tried to throw things, hit us and tore up her own house. He tried talking to her, and she went ballistic on him trying to fight the policeman. To make her stop he had to tase her and put her in cuffs. He called for the mental health examiner to come; ,by that time her eyes were glossy, and she was out of it.

They put her in a straitjacket and in the back of a van as they shipped her to a mental health facility. I informed the police that we could stay with a friend of the family for now, but I would be turning eighteen in a couple of days and wanted to see about getting custody of my baby brother. He gave me a couple of contacts and information to get me on the right path to make that happen. I was just relieved that we were rid of Aretha for good. That was a pain in the ass that I didn't have to worry about any longer. We got our stuff and headed back home not caring to even lock her door. Nosy ass neighbors were standing outside watching the whole ordeal take place, but I didn't care, it is what it is.

***

Today was my eighteenth birthday, and I was so excited. I had been counting down the days for a long time, and it was now finally here. I woke up to Khalil standing over me with a mini cake with the candles one and eight sticking in them. He had the biggest smile on his face as he said, "make a wish". I closed my eyes and did as I asked.

"It's too early for cake Khalil," I said giggling.

"I know ma that's why I did this," he went over to the table in our room and grabbed the breakfast platter that had food on it.

He cooked homemade blueberry waffles, beautiful scrambled eggs, turkey sausage, and cheese grits that was to die for. Khalil made me breakfast in bed, that was something that I never had before, and it made me feel good as hell on the inside. He was making me feel like a queen.

As I was eating my food, I looked around the room, and there were red heart-shaped balloons and shopping bags everywhere. Once I was done eating Khalil handed me an envelope that had my name on it. When I opened, there was a card on the inside that had a heartfelt message from Khalil.

"Today is your eighteenth birthday, and I am

glad that this day has finally come because you have been talking about it since the day I met you. LOL.

But nah for real, since the day I met you I've seen a different side of me. You bring out the best in me Lani and it's a blessing to have you in my life. Every moment that we spend together is one that I cherish. I love waking up to your beautiful face and button nose every morning.

I love the feeling of electricity that shoots through my body whenever you're in my arms. Everything with you just feels right. I'm saying all of that to say this, I promise to be by your side forever as your lover, protector, and friend. Love you ma.

-Khalil"

As I read the card, my heart felt warm, and my vision got blurry from tears of joy. Khalil kissed me on the lips as he pulled a white ring box from behind his back. When he opened the velvet box, there was a Timeless Elegance Ring in the color of Rose Gold. He also had the Rose Gold Pandora Bracelet to match that was already full of charms of all the things that I loved. It was so crazy because I've been admiring the ring and bracelet for a while now. I guess that was a plus to having a man that was observant. There weren't too many things that Khalil missed. He was now handing me another envelope, and I was speechless.

"Khalil this is too much baby."

"Nothing is too much for you queen."

I didn't know what I did to deserve this man, but I was thankful to have him. He was my king, and I was his queen. When I opened the envelope, there were eighteen one-hundred-dollar bills inside. I didn't know how to feel, I was happy, I felt so many emotions. I've had people to give me money before but never that much at once. I got all of the money out the envelope, but there was still something on the inside of it. It was a key. I looked lost as hell as I held the key up. Khalil just laughed at me as he grabbed my hand and we walked outside.

There was a black 2018 Nissan Altima fully loaded sitting in the driveway. I jumped up on him like a baby, and he just held me as I cried in his shirt. This man was showing out today with everything that he was doing for me. My brother was so happy for me that

I found love in a man like Khalil. I thanked my lucky stars daily because not too many women come across a guy like this. Let alone find this type of love. It was definitely one that didn't come by every day.

This was the most I got for my birthday in a long time. I was on cloud nine, and it was all thanks to Khalil. He promised me that I would wear a smile on my face and I be damned if I haven't been smiling since I opened my eyes this morning. I didn't want him to do anything else for me because he'd already done enough but if I knew Khalil the way I think I do I knew that he wasn't finished yet. I kissed him for what felt like an eternity. I kissed him over and over again, from his lips to all over his face.

I hopped inside of the car once I stopped kissing Khalil. In the cup holder, were two tickets. He was taking me to Atlanta to see my favorite singer K.Michelle, and that was the icing on the cake for me. I was so damn ready to go I just couldn't contain my excitement. I loved K so much, and Khalil knew it . When he said he would stop at nothing to keep a smile on my face, he didn't lie. The thought crossed my mind to ask Autumn to go with me, but I would have to think on that a little further. I feel that it was only right that Khalil go with me since he got the tickets for me. JJ, Khalil, and I went for a spin around the block in my car, and I was on cloud nine. This car was everything and more. It was my first car, and I never expected I would have a brand-new car and it was fully loaded with the six-inch touch screen, and Bose surrounds system throughout the car. We were riding down the street beating to Boosie. We just bust a couple of blocks around the hood just stunting in my new whip. I didn't want to stunt too hard, so we headed back to the house, so we could prepare to leave for Atlanta. Khalil asked me if I wanted Autumn to go to the show with me and I declined. I just wanted to spend my special day with love.

As we got back to the house, we started getting ready to hit the road. JJ was going with us too, so I was happy to get this day started. I put on some nice clothes since it was my birthday, I had to come through and show out. I put on a nice Nike purple t-shirt with light distressed blue jeans with the purple and green air max

95. I was feeling lovely as hell, I was looking good as hell, and my man made sure he kept reminding me. I was loving every moment of it. My guys were fresh as hell also. Khalil made sure that JJ's attire was just as fresh as his. Once we had everything, we needed for our weekend stay we were on our way to Atlanta. We made it there in a little over two hours. I loved being in the city, Atlanta was big as hell to me.

We checked into a suite at the Aloft hotel downtown. Khalil and I had a suite to ourselves and JJ was in the adjoining suite. We were going to eat before we went to the show. We had dinner at the Morton Steakhouse restaurant. The place was nice, and I loved the atmosphere. The employees were so welcoming and made you feel so comfortable. We were seated immediately because my guy already made reservations for the three of us. We started with the Short Rib Steak Tacos for an appetizer. We all ate as we waited for our entrees to arrive at the table. The Porterhouse steak was to die for, and the Caesar salad was tasty as hell to my taste buds. The three of us laughed and talked the entire dinner, and I was feeling the love from both of them. For dessert I decided on a New York Cheesecake, Khalil had a Key-Lime Pie, and JJ had Morton's Legendary Hot Chocolate Cake. The cheesecake was melting in my mouth. I was having fun at the restaurant, but I couldn't lie, I was ready to get back to the hotel to get dressed for the concert. I was beyond excited to see my girl K, and Khalil blessed me with front row seats and a VIP Pass. He knew how excited I was, so he paid the bill and left the waiter a generous tip, and we left the restaurant.

The fact that Khalil was going to the show with me made me even more excited. Some men would prefer Boosie or Gates shows, but my man was going with me to make sure I had a good time. K had music that men could vibe to too, but even if she didn't how could you not love her. I have been rocking with her music for a while now, and I was a true fan. I knew the lyrics to every song, and that always made for a good show.

My hair was falling pretty as my twist out came out just right. I wore a part on the left side of my hair, and that gave my fro the perfect edge. As always, my makeup was natural, but my highlight was popping. I wore my favorite chocolate matte lipstick on my lips. My attire was a Nude Kara Bandage Dress. Christian Louboutin So Full Kate Studded Metallic Leather Red Sole Booties complimented my feet. Khalil did his thing with the shoes; the rhinestones and spikes made the booties bad as hell. He knew just what my taste was and made sure I didn't half step on my special day. I wore a gold choker around my neck, sprayed some Dolce & Gabanna perfume on, and I was set. I just sat down on the chaise and watched my man as he continued to get dressed. I admired his handsomeness; he had a fresh cut that complimented his dimples. He was looking all GQ; he wore a cream-colored button-down shirt that was close to the color of my dress with some black slacks that were crisp as hell with the crease. He wore a Gucci leather belt that had the double g's in the front. On his feet were black suede Colonnaki Velours Christian slippers. He dabbed a little of his Dolce & Gabbana Light Blue Intense cologne on, and he was now ready. We had JJ snap us a couple of pictures before we left the hotel. We were a sexy ass couple if I must say so myself. Our outfits complimented one another.

We made it to the Fox Theatre in no time. Khalil opened my door for me as he always did. He held my hand as we walked to our seats. I was already having a good time, and the show hadn't even started yet. She had some small artists open up for her, they were straight, but I was just ready to see who I came for. When she finally came on the stage, I went crazy. She looked gorgeous as hell with her ruby red unit. I was singing along to all of the songs even the breakup songs like I didn't have my man standing right next to me. I was having the time of my life, and honestly, this was my first concert ever. This day will forever be embedded in my mind; my eighteenth birthday was something special. I had the chance to go to one of my favorite singer's shows and even had the opportunity to get a picture with her backstage. Just talking to her made my day. She was so humble and down to earth. She didn't treat me like a fan. Instead I felt like an old friend of hers. The feeling was indescribable.

Once the show was over Khalil, and I just

walked downtown hand in hand as we went sightseeing. I was having such a good time, and he was making me feel like the most beautiful girl in the world. I couldn't stop staring at my promise ring he gave me. Just replaying back, the moment he gave it to me and the words that he said to me made my heart feel butterflies.

"Khalil... I've never met anyone like you before. You give me this unfamiliar feeling, and it's hard as hell to explain it, but all I know is that when I'm with you, everything just feels right. Every time I'm in your presence I feel butterflies. You are truly heaven sent, I thank god the day he put you in my path. I'm so glad that I went to that gas station and party that night," I said laughing with tears in my eyes. This feeling was crazy as hell, and I knew exactly what Queen Naija was talking about in her song 'Butterflies'. When we made it to the car, I played the song from my phone and let it play through the Bluetooth speakers so that Khalil could hear it. I wanted him to listen to the lyrics because, for the words that I couldn't find, Queen knew just what to say to describe every emotion I was feeling towards this man of mine.

I don't wanna fall so fast

But I'm open

They always say that good things never last

And I know 'cause I've been broken

I'm tryin' to protect my heart

But you're making it so hard

And I guess it's safe to say

You take my pain away

And I just wanna hold you all night long

Whenever I'm around you, nothing's wrong

I'm hoping that you'll always be around

You got me on a high, I don't wanna come down

And I love it, I love it (these butterflies)

Yeah I love it, I love it (I'm on a high)

Yeah, I love it, I love it

And I just wanna love on you (ooh)

I looked in his eyes as I sung the words from the depth of my soul. He held my hand up to his mouth and kissed the back of it as he drove to the hotel. I loved this song, and she put my feelings into words. When we got back to the suite, JJ was already knocked out. When we walked into our portion of the suite there were rose petals everywhere and on the bed there were petals that were shaped in the form of a heart. On the table, there was some wine and chocolate covered strawberries. This man went above and beyond for me on my birthday. All I could do was hug and kiss him. I was getting ready to show him just how much I appreciated everything that he was doing for me. I was going to make passionate love to my man all night long until the morning comes.

Chapter 12

KHALIL

We were back in the gump, and a nigga was tired as hell. I was just glad that I succeeded at putting a smile on baby girl's face. That was my only objective. I had been planning shit since I found out when her birthday was. At first, I didn't know what exactly I was going to do for her, but I started paying more and more attention to her. I started paying attention to the things she searched on the internet, the items she eyed whenever she was scrolling on social media. Seems like I did everything right because she smiled the entire day, even cried but they were tears of joy. Just to hear her express her love for me made a nigga feel something on the inside. The way she was telling me that she felt about me, the feelings were mutual on my end. Lani was my everything and more.

Ever since the day she walked in my life, and we started spending time together, my days have been brighter. I didn't feel alone out here in these streets anymore. True I had Hassan, but it was a whole different type of loyalty that I got from her. She was my lady, and I loved her. Shit with us transpired so fast but I once heard someone say that when is real, you'd know I knew for the jump. I never doubted that she was the one for me. The way I cared for her, the lengths that I would go for her told me everything that I needed to know. She was the one that I had been waiting for and now that I had her no other man will ever have the opportunity. I wasn't letting her go at all, we were in this thing for eternity, and I knew that she would be my wife one day. I already treated her as such because in my eyes she was; we just didn't have the papers to state it just yet.

The drive from Atlanta had me a little drained on top of all that good loving Lani had put on me all weekend. She was showing her gratitude from sun up to sun down, and a nigga wasn't mad at that at all. We had been lounging around in the bed since we've been back. We were cuddled up watching a movie, and I eventually dozed off keeping Lani up. I woke up when

I no longer felt Lani presence in the bed lying beside me. I could hear her having a conversation with someone, but I couldn't seem to recognize the voice. When I walked in the living room, there was an older like woman standing in the doorway. She wasn't necessarily old, but she was in her late thirties or early forties at least. She kind of looked familiar to me, but I couldn't put my finger on it. She had thick black hair that was shoulder length and was pressed bone straight with a part on the side. She was a pretty woman, appearing to weigh around 170 pounds. She was dressed nice in a blue jean coat with denim pants and some caramel colored Ugg boots. I peeped all of this from the hallway where no one could see me standing there. I guess it was just my Hitta instincts. I walked up to the door behind Lani as I towered over her small frame, placing my hand on the door to open it up further as I moved her behind me.

"Yo Lani, who this?"

"Khalil...she says..." before she had a chance to finish her statement the woman fainted, I caught her before her head had a chance to hit the hard concrete.

I was thinking to myself what the hell was going on and who was this woman that wasfainting at my door. Immediately Lani and I helped her into the house and set her on the couch. Lani went into the closet to get a wash rag, she wet it with cold water and placed it on the woman's forehead. I went into the kitchen to get a bottle of water when I noticed that she was waking up. Lani never did tell me who the woman was, she insisted that we waited until she woke up and let her tell me herself. That was the purpose of me getting the water, so she could wet her throat, and nothing would be holding her back. When she finally opened her eyes, she looked directly into mine, and she broke down crying. I was lost and confused, who was this woman sitting on my couch looking into my face crying?

"This is extremely hard for me, and I'm trying my best to find the words to say to you. Khalil, I am your mother, my name is Connie.

"Mother?! I never had one of those." I said. I could feel the muscles tighten up in my jaw as I spoke. This whole ordeal was blowing me. I had been an orphan until I was fifteen years old, and nowhere was this woman was claiming to be my mother. As far as I was concerned, I didn't have any relatives at all. I had been in this cold world all alone, and as the years went by, I have grown to accept that. I went from foster family to foster family, and I never felt that I belonged to any of those family. I was the stepchild that no one ever wanted; they just took me in to reap the benefits. I was pissed as I stormed to the door and opened it for shorty letting her know that she had to leave.

"Khalil please just hear her out babe. I believe she is your mom. You're her spitting image Khalil, can't you see that."

I paid no attention to the woman, her face did resemble mines. I had her complexion, I was really the male version of her, and it was crazy that she was sitting right here in my living room. Never in a million years did I think I would ever see this day. I didn't notice how much we resembled one another until now. I thought that I knew her from somewhere, from around the way or maybe in passing but it was just really like me looking into the mirror.

Lani always knew what to say to make me

soften up, and she was the only reason I calmed down a little bit. I listened to her as I shut the door and I was going to give the woman the chance to tell me why she was here, and how did she find me. I needed something to drink myself because I knew this was going to be a lot to take in and I couldn't necessarily say that my heart or mind was prepared for it. I went into the kitchen and fixed me a glass of Grand Marnier on the rocks as I took a shot before going into the living room to join Connie and Lani. I never thought in a million years that I would see this day and it never crossed my mind honestly, but here we were. I was just glad that I didn't have to face this moment alone. Lani was right by my side just as she always had been since day one. She sat beside me and held my hand tightly as we sat across from Connie.

"We're listening," I said to her.

"Khalil don't be rude."

"I'm sorry. Can you just give me the rundown on how you found me and everything Ms. Connie. I'm sorry if I'm coming off a bit harsh, but I'm sure you understand that this caught me completely off guard and is a lot for me to take in"?

"I understand where you're coming from sweetie, I really do. I don't even know where to begin, but I guess I have to start somewhere, so why not start from the beginning. Well, I was a young girl who was in love at the tender age of fifteen with an older guy from the hood. He was a big-time drug dealer in Milwaukee, and my dad didn't approve. He was a hustler, but when it came down to me, he was as gentle as a feather. I was his world, and he was mine. I got pregnant with you at the age of fifteen and my parents' shitted bricks, they were very dissatisfied that their daughter was out being fast and got a child as a result.

They resented me, they were ashamed of me, and they made sure that I knew it every day. They were so busy trying to uphold an image and appear to be the best parents that gave their child the best education that money could buy. They never once stopped to think what I wanted. Did I want to live in the suburbs in a five-bedroom house and it was only three of us, and they shared a room. They were both over the top and tried to keep up with their colleagues or be better than them. The only good thing about my pregnancy was that I knew that I had a healthy baby boy living on the inside of me. They never once stopped to think about how the things they were doing and saying were affecting me.

I was depressed the entire duration of my pregnancy. Initially, they would have made me get an abortion, but I was too far along when they found out. So, I carried you to full term, and once I had you, they forced me to give you up for adoption, and they moved me to Missouri to live with my aunt. They made me cut all ties with your father and shortly after I left, I heard he was killed. I knew that he was living a very dangerous lifestyle, but I believe that my father played a part in his death. I had both of the loves of my life swept away from me in an instant, and it broke me. I didn't know what to do with myself. I hated them for that every day of my life. I was lost, empty, and broken. I carried you for nine months and as soon as you escaped my womb you were taken from me. I fell into a state of depression then, not knowing where you were or what kind of hands you would end up in. I never stopped looking for you, Khalil."

"So where have you been these last couple of years? Since you were grown where did you go? Did you stay with your aunt? How did you find me now? I know I'm asking a lot, but these are questions that I need to be answered."

"When I turned eighteen I moved around from here and there. Living in shelters and different shit. Due to my depression I was in for years, I started doing all kind of things to make myself feel better. I was stripping for a while and robbing niggas. After almost getting killed in the process I left that life alone. I moved to South Carolina, and I got settled there. I had a good customer service job as a waitress at a local Denny's. I worked there all the while until I came here. I got involved with a man by the name of Ronnie. In the beginning, he was my night and shining armor, but quickly he showed me another side of him. He treated me like a queen trying to bribe me with nice things and doing all types of shit to win me over. It had been so long since I even had some male attention and I felt that he was genuine with everything that he was doing for me. I should have known that it all was too good to be true.

Over time he became possessive, wanting to control where I went, what I wear, the way I styled my hair, all the way down to the smell of my perfume. The possessiveness turned into abuse. I didn't know what to do, every time I tried to fight back the beatings got worse, so eventually, I just started taking them. Every day I prayed for a way out, but it always seemed easier said than done. I was tired as hell of getting my ass whooped every day for little to nothing. I hired a PI to find you, and it has taken some years, but finally, I located you. I saved up all of my checks and tips and when I had enough a got me a bus ticket to Alabama. I got dressed in my work uniform, and Ronnie dropped me off like he normally did. When I saw him leave the parking lot, I exited the back of the restaurant and called a Lyft to take me to the bus station, and now I'm here. There is no doubt in my mind that he isn't tearing up the city looking for me. I just pray that he gives up on finding me."

Lani and I both sat there quietly as we listened

to her intently. She had just said a mouthful, and I was taking it all in bit by bit. It was crazy that this was happening all of a sudden, but sometimes life just dropped bombs on you like that. As she talked about her childhood and being pregnant with me made me soften up to her. I hated that she had to endure that type of pain and hatred from her own parents. I could tell how much I meant to her and also how much her and my father meant to one another. Life was so crazy because I remember growing up resenting my parents thinking that they didn't want me. In reality, they never had a chance to be in my life. That hurt to know that my own grandparents; my blood didn't even want me around. It was some selfish ass people in this world. I felt for Connie because even in her adult life she was still experiencing hardships. I hated that she was in an abusive relationship and the only way out of it was to skip town and run away. Even though everything she just said to me was new, I felt the constant urge to be there for her and help her in any way that I could.

It was a little easier to look at her now because I knew everything that she had to go through. I don't feel that she would have given me up if she had a chance, but at that age, there was nothing she could do. If the circumstances were different than we would have been together all of these years and who knows? Maybe my father would have been here and would have had the opportunity to raise me. I was a firm believer that everything happens for a reason though. If it wasn't meant for us to meet after all of these years then she wouldn't have been here right now. As she told me about the abuse, it immediately infuriated me, but I was just glad that she was here with me now and I would do everything in my power to protect her just as I did Lani and JJ. She was still crying as her emotions were getting the best of her. I pulled her into my embrace and hugged her tightly, and an unfamiliar feeling overcame me. My emotions got the best of me and tears started falling rapidly from my eyes. It had been so long since I even shed a tear. I can't even remember the last time I cried. Lani had never seen me cry before, and it made her tear up to see me in such a vulnerable state.

Eventually, the tears became tears of joy. I was

overjoyed to have my mother here with me. I let her know that she had somewhere to stay and she didn't have to worry about anything, I had her. Normally I would take more precautions before doing something as drastic as moving someone who was practically a stranger into my house. I didn't feel like I had to do that in this circumstance, after all, she was my mother. The lady carried me in her womb for nine months, this was the least I could do to repay her. I couldn't have her out on the streets easily accessible to the nigga she was running from. Granted he was probably still in South Carolina, but I was the only one that she had here in Bama.

We spent the rest of the night getting acquainted and getting to know each other a little more. I caught her up on how I was bounced around as a kid and how I never really felt wanted. She hated that she missed so much of my life, but I reminded her that it wasn't her fault. As we continued our conversation, I realized that Connie never did say anything else about her parents. I was curious to know if they tried to keep a relationship with her over the years even after making her give up her baby. I asked her about them and got the shock of my life when she said that she killed them. I couldn't even judge her knowing everything that they put her through and all that was taken away from her. I guess the apple didn't fall too far from the tree. I couldn't tell her that though, but at least I knew where I got my killer instincts from. It was already in my blood.

I was taking down this cognac tonight, I needed a strong, stiff drink. So much was on my mental and I was still processing the whole thing. I watched from the kitchen bar as Connie and Lani had girl talk and talked like mother and daughter. They hit it off immediately, and it made my heart smile. I could tell that they already cared for one another and in the future, they would have an unbreakable bond. Just knowing that she was my mother would instantly make Lani love her, that was the kind of heart she had. It's like they were developing a mother and daughter bond and that motherly bond was something that Lani didn't get the chance to experience for long. I never even had that opportunity, so it would be new to me.

I went into my laundry room and grabbed some

clean covers and sheets to make up my extra bedroom for Connie. I knew that she must have been tired from that long bus ride. I just wanted her to be as comfortable as possible during her stay. She would stay with us, we had more than enough room, and I knew that Lani wouldn't mind her being here. They were laughing and talking in the living room like old friends. It was getting late, so I showed Connie to the guest room and let her know that if she needed anything that she could ask me or Lani.

Lani and I laid in bed in the dark. I held Lani in my arms as I stared at the ceiling fan twirling around. I was lost in my thoughts as today's events replayed in my head. I kissed Lani on the forehead, she was a strong woman, and she always stood by my side. I appreciated her for always having my back and being there when I needed her the most. I wouldn't have been able to get through this day without her. I was lucky to have her. I kissed her goodnight, and we both fell asleep.

***

I woke up to an empty bed and the smell of

breakfast. I just smiled as I heard chatter and laughter from my mother and Lani. I knew that Lani was probably in the kitchen preparing a feast right about now. The way that my stomach was growling, I hopped out of bed with the quickness to get myself together. I went into the bathroom to take a quick shower and handle my hygiene. I got dressed in something comfortable, putting on gym shorts and a wife beater.

I went into the kitchen and had a seat at the breakfast bar alongside my mother. Her and Lani were already munching on some bacon.

"Good morning ladies."

"Good morning handsome," Lani said and came around and kissed me on the lips.

"Good morning Khalil," my mother said to me with a smile on her face.

The both of them were in a good mood this morning. I noticed that my mother had on the same clothes from the night before. I made a mental note to ask Lani to go with me to take her to get a couple of things to make her stay more comfortable. After we sat down and ate breakfast together, Lani and I went into our bedroom to get dressed so we could leave the house. When we were finished getting dressed, we walked into the living room to see Connie sitting on the couch watching TV. We all headed to the car, and I made sure that the security system was alarmed before leaving the house. I just asked Lani where to, and I lead the way like a chauffeur. I was letting the ladies do all of the shopping, I was just swiping the card. We went to Walmart to get the necessities like towels, soap, and all the other things a woman would need. I got her all kind of clothes for outings and some just to be comfortable in the house. By now she had everything she needed, so I decided to take them to get lunch.

We decided to go to Olive Garden for lunch. Our waitress greeted us and seated us in a nice cozy booth in the back of the restaurant next to the window. We ordered our drinks as we had a longer look at the menu trying to decide what we wanted to eat. The waitress came back, and we ordered our meals. I decided on some shrimp fettuccine alfredo, and the women had similar meals. The garden salad and breadsticks were hitting. We stayed at the restaurant for at least two and a half hours, just sitting there talking and being too full to move. I paid the bill and tipped the waitress before proceeding to leave the restaurant.

Once we were back home, we dropped Connie off before Lani, and I left to go see Hassan. JJ was there, and I asked him to keep an eye on her. If either of them needed us while we were out, they had our numbers so that they could reach us. Today we were going to give Lani a little target practice with different guns. That was the main training she would need because everything else was really common sense. I had her in that area, and I would make sure she had all of the knowledge she would need to be able to move strategically in this game. When we arrived at Hassan's crib, we walked all the way to the back of the mansion. He had his gun range set up in a secluded area of his house. The shit was neat as hell, and he didn't have to leave the house to get a little practice in if he wanted to. He had the guns laid out, and we were ready to get started. Lani was excited about the whole ordeal, I think she was just happy about the fact that she was starting her training. I knew that she was more than capable of shooting a gun, I just wanted her to be a skilled shooter. She needed to be able to shoot from long range and up close. You never know how a hit would go down so whatever way it needed to be executed, that's just how we would have to do it.

We started her off shooting pistols, and if I had to say so myself, she had a perfect aim. She was hitting straight head shots, and I was amazed. The girl was a natural and she could do that shit with her eyes closed. Hassan was shocked by how good of a shooter she was, but I already had experienced it before. She had target practice for about three hours, and I was sure she had seen enough of this for the day. We sat down and had a quick conversation with Hassan and then we were on our way home.

When we arrived home, my mother and JJ were sitting in the living room watching an action movie. Lani and I joined them because it seemed interesting as it had them drawn in. As I looked around at the faces that are in my living room now, I noticed that we sort of formed our own little family. I loved everyone in this room, and I would do anything for them. Even though

I just met my mom I felt the same way about her, after all, she was my blood.

Chapter 13

RONNIE

I dropped Connie off at work before heading in to do my typical nine to five at the tire shop. I had her on my mind real heavy today for some reason. I remember the first day I met her. Me and a few of my coworkers stopped by the diner where she worked at for a bite to eat on our lunch break. I admired her as she went around from table to table asking the customers if they were good or if they needed anything else. She was beautiful to me. Her smile lit up the dimly lit diner. I was supposed to be looking over the menu to decide on what I wanted to eat, but I couldn't seem to stop staring at her. I guess she could feel me staring at her because she looked up and gave me an innocent smile. I just wined as I placed my face back into the menu. I finally decided on a simple cheeseburger and fries. I was just waiting for her to come take our order. She maneuvered around the diner liked she owned it. I was sure that her personality made her a lot of money in tips.

"How y'all doing? What can I start y'all off with to drink?"She asked me and the fellas.

"I'll have a sweet tea," I said and the rest of the fellas gave her their drink orders.

She wrote everything down on her little notepad. She left and came back with our drinks, and she then wrote down our food orders. I continuously flirted with her while I was at the diner. She just kept smiling and being polite. I went for the kill and asked her for her phone number. I could tell that she was a little hesitant about giving it to me, so I just put my number in her phone instead. I left her a generous tip on the table, and we left to go back to work. Something about her just made me instantly drawn to her. I could tell that she was a little standoffish, but that didn't stop me from trying to pursue her. I put my number in her phone not knowing if she would ever hit me up.

I was watching the Cowboys play a game when my phone started to ring. It was an unknown number, so I immediately knew it was her. I answered the phone with the quickness, and I heard the sweet sound of her voice. We talked for a while and made plans to meet up for lunch. The next day we met up and ate lunch together. She was a nice lady and a real sweetheart. From that day we started hanging out more and more. We started doing everything together, and we quickly became an item.

I had been single for some time before meeting her. I was divorced after being with my children's mother for nine years. Shit with her just got old overtime, and I just couldn't stand the sight of her anymore. Every day we were constantly fussing and fighting, I was tired of going through the same bullshit every day. My kids were the main reason I stuck around. I just wanted them to have that family image that I never had growing up. I wanted them to see their mother and father together and not living in separate households. I got off of work early one day and went by the flower boutique to get her some roses in an effort to surprise her. When I walked in the house, it was smelling good as hell as candles were burning all over the house.

Imagine my surprise when I reached our bedroom door, and I saw my ex-wife on top of another man riding him for dear life. I lost all my cool as I threw her on the floor and broke the vase that held the roses on homeboy's head. We were tussling and making all kind of holes in the wall. She was crying hysterically, but I paid it no mind as I was beating the fuck out of her little boy toy. I pulled my gun out on him, and he was scared shitless. I gave him the opportunity to get out of my house before I killed him.

It took everything in me not to shoot him in his head. I started taking my anger out on her as I beat her mercifully. I just couldn't believe she had the audacity to bring another nigga into the home where I pay the bills at. That night I packed my shit and left. I stayed away for weeks because I was scared of what I might do if I ever saw her again. I realized that I was neglecting my kids, so I came around for that purpose and that purpose only. At the end of the day, I was a grown man, so it was a must that I be a father to my kids. So, I did what any man would do, I took her to court, so I could get visitation rights for my girls. The court decided that we alternate holidays and I got them every other weekend. Her, and I didn't have a relationship at all, I spoke to her solely when it came down to my kids.

So, you see I was still carrying a lot of baggage from my past marriage when I met Connie. I knew that I wasn't fully healed from the situation, but I wanted to move on, I needed someone to make me forget her. Just the thought of the woman I loved and decided to make my wife; living the good life with another nigga fucked with me on the daily. Granted, I knew shit between us hadn't been sweet in a while, but I still had love for her. We had history together, years invested in our relationship. She was the mother of my kids, so I'll always have a soft spot for her.

I felt like meeting Connie was right on time. She was a welcoming distraction to get my mind off of my ex. As time went on things got serious between us quickly. We moved in with one another after three months of dating. She was feeling me, and I was feeling her. It was like instant chemistry between us. Things between us were good, and I was happy to have her in my life. I could tell that she was much different than what I was used to. She looked out for me and always made sure I was straight. She catered to my every need. She cooked, cleaned, washed a nigga draws. Anything I needed she was always at my beck and call, I was glad that I took a chance on getting to know her. She was just what I needed after going through what I went through.

A nigga got comfortable rather quickly. Over time I started to feel my jealous tendencies flare up. I don't know why but I just started thinking what if she found someone better and wanted to leave me like the last woman did. I started picking her up and dropping her off at work. I wanted to be up under her every chance I got. I never wanted her to have too much space out of fear that she would find better. One day I was drunk and reminiscing on what happened to me in my past, and I put my hands on her. She did nothing the liquor just had me fucked up. It became routine, I started beating her for little to nothing. If her pants were too tight, if I didn't like the lipstick she wore, any little thing would set me off. I just had a possessive mindset, and I wanted her to do everything just the way I wanted. I don't know why, but that's just the way I was when it came to her. I just didn't want to be alone again, so that was my sick little way of keeping her on track, so she wouldn't stray away.

I know she probably thought I didn't love or care about her, but I really did. I just had a fucked-up way of showing it. My trust issues were all fucked up, I had insecurities out the ass. Connie never did anything to me for me not to trust her, but I just couldn't. I had a tracking device set up on her phone, but I didn't need it because she did nothing but went to work and came home to be with me on the daily.

"Yo Ronnie, let's do this last car together so we can dip out and close shop for the day."

"That's a bet Mark. That'll be good timing, so I can be on time to get Connie from work," I said.

We finished putting brand new tires and rotating them on our last car of the day. Once we were done closing up the shop, I headed over to the diner to pick up my woman. I pulled into the parking lot and parked in a vacant spot close to the entrance of the shop. Looking at the time on the car radio I noticed that I had ten minutes to spare before Connie got off. I started scrolling on Facebook to kill the time. I was so caught up watching funny videos from Facebook comedians that I didn't realize that thirty minutes had passed already. She would normally be strolling out any moment now. I gave her five more minutes thinking maybe she had to do a little more cleaning or something. When another five minutes passed, I got out of the car and entered the shop. Looking around the diner I didn't see her anywhere in sight. Noticing one of her coworkers that she talked to on the regular, I greeted her and asked her was Connie in the back.

"I haven't seen Connie today Ron, you sure she was on the schedule to work today?"

"Yeah Meaca, I dropped her off this morning. It's impossible for her not to be here."

"Well I don't know what to tell you," she said as she rolled her eyes and her neck at the same time.

Now I was pissed off because someone was trying to play games with me and I didn't have time for that shit today. I had a long ass day of work, and I just wanted to be at home drinking on me a beer as I relaxed on my couch. But today out of all days was the day they chose to test my gangsta. My blood started boiling, and I was becoming more pissed off by the second. Before I knew it, I grabbed Meaca by the neck and started choking the life out of her. She was losing conscious by the minute, I had to quickly realize that I was in a public place and I wasn't trying to catch a DV. It was too many eyes in there at that time. I let her go as I watch her struggle to catch her breath. I went to the back of the diner, into the kitchen area as I looked around for Connie, but she wasn't in there. I looked in the bathrooms, searching each stall but she was still nowhere to be found. I had come to the conclusion that she wasn't here. I don't know where the fuck she was, but she better turn up sooner or later if she knew what was good for her.

Chapter 14

DEON

Autumn had been blowing my phone up all day, and I had been ignoring her because I was out making plays. I didn't know what was so important that she had to talk to me about, but she was irritating the fuck out of me. Her ass probably wanted some dick, I would have to check her ass later. I was on the block as usual slanging and shit. The money was flowing, and business was great right now. The only problem I had was that my little runner JP had been giving me the runaround, playing with my money and shit. The nigga was short with my money, and I gave him the opportunity to pay me my money by midnight a while back. It was weeks later, damn near a couple of months and I hadn't seen or heard from the nigga yet. I wasn't chasing behind his ass because I had a whole lot of other shit going on, but his time was coming. No one would fuck with my money and get away with it.

He had been hiding out pretty good, no one had heard anything from him in a minute. That was cool though because he couldn't stay hiding forever. He would see me soon, and that was for sure. When I was done handling my business on the streets, I left and headed to Wing Master's to get me some food to grub on. I ordered a twenty-piece lemon pepper wet with a large lemonade to wash it down with. The girl that was working the drive-thru window was a little cutie. When she handed me my receipt, I handed it right back to her.

"Why don't you write your number down on there, so I can call you sometimes," she just blushed and started writing it down for me. She handed me the receipt back, and I smiled at shorty. I let her know that I would be hitting her line soon before pulling off.

That was an easy ass score, but at the same time, it was never really hard for me. I was a handsome ass nigga and could have any bitch I wanted for real. Autumn thought she was my main squeeze, but I just fucked with her for the convenience. Lani wasn't giving me any play, so I fucked with her hoe ass friend instead. I guess she was all in love with that pretty boy or whatever but one thing for sure was that he wasn't me. He had a nice whip or whatever, but I know that little Foot Locker gig couldn't afford all of that lavish shit that Lani liked to have.

Even though she was with him, that didn't stop me from thinking about her every day. Hell, I even think about her when I'm with Autumn. I always thought in the back of my mind that when she chose someone to fuck with on the heavy tip that it would be me. I guess I was sadly mistaken. Maybe she never really felt the way that I did about her. Sometimes I think that it's my fault that she got away like that. I probably should have been a man and came out and confessed my true feelings for her. That was just a hard thing for me because I never really knew how to express myself. I always felt like it made me looked weak. The ringing of my iPhone snapped me out of my thoughts. Looking down at the caller id I got irritated all over.

"What the fuck is up Autumn? You've been

blowing my shit up all day."

"I'm sorry Dee, I just need to talk to you about something important."

"Give me five minutes man, I'm in traffic now. I'll swing through."

"Okay," she said. I hung up in the middle of her getting the words out.

I began to wonder what the damn urgency was. One thing for sure was that her ass knew how to worry somebody. At times she could be worrisome as fuck, and sometimes she was good ass company. When she wasn't on all that extra shit, I didn't mind her being in my presence.

I had my plate of wings opened up sitting on my passenger seat, so I could have easy access to them as I was driving. A nigga was hungry as fuck because I hadn't eaten anything all day. As I was turning on Autumn's street. I closed my plate up and tied up the plastic bag that it was in. When I stopped in front of her house, she came out. I was going to meet her on the porch, but I thought against it not wanting to be seen. I unlocked my car door and moved the plate off the passenger seat so that she could get in. She had a very solemn look on her face and it kind of worried me. I never saw her looked so pitiful before, so I was curious about what was up with her. The more she just sat there like she didn't know what to say I began to wonder did Lani find out about us or something. But then I thought nah because she would have told me that over the phone. I just sat there letting her find her words so that she could speak. A tear fell from her eyes, and I knew then that it was something deep.

"Deon, I'm pregnant," she said sadly.

"Come again!?"

"Nigga you heard what the fuck I said. I'm pregnant, and it's yours, so what the fuck are we going to do about this shit."

"Man, what makes you think that it is mines?"

"Because contrary to what you may believe you're the only nigga I've been laying down with."

"Fuck man!! When did you find out?

"Today."

That little piece of news fucked my head up for real. I wouldn't know what the fuck to do with a child.

I was too deep in the streets to even think about raising one. I had got caught slipping. I don't know why but the first person that I thought about was Lani. I knew that would hurt her to know that her best friend was pregnant by me. I'm sure she kept that to herself because everyone would want to know who the father was. I got my head together and had her call to make an appointment with an OBGYN to see how far along she was. She only did a home test so for all I knew she probably wasn't pregnant. Her appointment was the next day at three p.m. so for right now I just preferred to be alone, so I could gather my thoughts. I let her know that she could hit my line if she needed something.

I went home and got in the hot shower lost in my thoughts. I can't believe that this shit was happening right now. I was starting to feel like I had entirely too much on my plate. First the shit with Lani fuckin with that nigga, JP playing around with my money, and now this shit about Autumn being pregnant. Don't get me wrong I knew what we were doing could result in her getting pregnant, but it never really crossed my mind. I never asked was she on birth control before I started bussing all in her. I had been acting real reckless lately, and it's nobody's fault but mine. I was letting my emotions control my actions, and that was never a good thing to do. Lani had my mind fucked up, and I just couldn't seem to shake this bullshit she was on. I was in the shower longer than expected. The shower was my thinking place, but sometimes I got lost in there. I got out and wrapped the towel around my body.

Walking into the living room I already had a couple of pre-rolled blunts sitting on the coffee table. I went into the kitchen and grabbed two Corona's out of the fridge. I sat on the couch, kicking my feet up on the ottoman. I lit the blunt and let the haze take me away. I had to think of something quickly to diffuse this situation. I was praying that she wasn't too far along, so we could have an abortion. That was the only like mind thing to do. I wasn't ready for a kid, and she was still in school. Neither of us had time for a child, and I was man enough to know that it was something that I simply wasn't ready for. I don't know how she would feel about the whole abortion thing, but I prayed to God that we were on the same page, I needed us to be.

I tried my best to get some shut eye before the sun came up. I knew that it would be a little hard with so much on my mental, but it was worth a try. The next day I woke up feeling a little refreshed and ready to face the day. It was early as hell, so I handled my hygiene and hit the block like I would do on any other day. I would leave in enough time to pick Autumn up from school and take her to the doctor's office. I had faith that everything was going to work out in my favor, so I wasn't tripping off of anything at this point. I thought back on that time where I carelessly slept with her without a condom, and I realized that she couldn't have been that far along.

That made me feel a whole lot better about the situation. I knew that we should be able to get rid of it before the baby had a chance to start developing. I hugged the block from morning until evening. Business was booming today, and I didn't want to leave, but I knew I had some serious shit that required my attention. I prayed that Autumn wasn't on her bullshit as I made my way to her school. I parked in the parking lot and sent her a text to let her know that I was outside. Five minutes later she came through the double doors of the school.

I just looked at her and admired her beauty. She wasn't an ugly girl at all, she just had some fucked-up ways. I really did too because we both was on some fucked up shit, so I really couldn't judge her. She owed Lani more loyalty than I did, she was her best friend. Women expect shit like this from niggas, but she was just on some snake shit. It was so crazy because we have been creeping behind Lani's back for months now and she still had no clue. Sometimes I felt bad, but I still didn't stop. That's why we were on our way to the doctor's office trying to find about the duration of her pregnancy. This shit was crazy as hell.

We arrived at the doctor's office about fifteen minutes later. I didn't want to get out because I knew how motherfuckers talk and the word would be out in no time. I guess it was just a risk I had to take because I didn't want her to have to face it on her own. After all, I played a part in making this child as well, even if it wasn't planned. I never once thought about her having my child or her being my baby mother. That wasn't what I wanted, I was just simply enjoying life and having fun right now, that's all.

I waited in the waiting room as she went into the back and had her ultrasound, and everything done. I didn't want people to know that it was my child. I just wanted to seem as if I was giving her a friendly ride to the doctor. Montgomery was small as hell, and I knew in no time this would be around the city. It didn't take long, and the visit was over. I walked out behind her, and neither of us said anything until we reached the car. She was only four weeks, and that was music to my ears. I hated to have her get rid of the baby, but the timing was just off.

"I don't know how you feel about the whole thing, but I think we should terminate your pregnancy."

"Deon I already knew that you would say that. I knew you didn't want to have a baby by me...I get it. No need to say anything else."

"It's not like that Autumn, don't take it like that.

It's just bad timing, you haven't even finished school yet. You know that I'm deep in the streets, I can't bring a child into this world with the life I'm living. Now just isn't the time shorty. Maybe if it would've been under different circumstances, different timing it could have worked out, but now is not the time," I said giving her all types of false hope.

I didn't mean to I just had to butter her up, so she could agree to the abortion. I was going to pay for the whole thing, she wouldn't have to worry about coming up with the money for it. Finally, she started to see things from my point of view. I could tell that she was a little sad about it, but I would make it up to her in no time. She insisted that of we were going to do it we might as well get it out the way. I wasn't necessarily in a rush, but I could understand her wanting to get it over and done with. We traveled an hour out of the city to have the procedure done. I knew that no one knew me in this city, so I felt that it was okay for me to get out and be there for support. I knew that just asking her to have the abortion was asking a lot of her so the least I could do was go inside with her and hold her hand.

The look on her face was enough to almost make me call the whole thing off, but I just couldn't bring myself to do it. The shit was fucking with my head. I didn't know if I was making a mistake or not. If not, I knew that I would have to face that karma in the near future because the damage was already done. The procedure was done quicker than I thought. I guess that was a good thing, well at least for Autumn. She came out of the operation room wearing an empty expression on her face. I knew that must have been hard for her by the energy she was giving off. I tried to make her smile as I hugged her from the back as we walked to the car. I just wanted her to cheer up. When we were back in the city, I pulled into the Bruster's Ice Cream drive-thru. I knew that she loved her cookies and cream ice cream in a waffle cone. I ordered her one of those and got me one but with butter pecan. That little gesture made her ease up a little bit. I was going to break down this little wall she had built up to try to keep me out.

I cared about Autumn, I did. I just didn't care about her the way that she wanted me to. I had love for the chick. We have known each other since we were jits. We practically grew up together. Even as youngins I always had a little thing for Lani, overlooking Autumn. Who would've known that years later that she would be the one that I would lay down with. It's funny how life pans out sometimes. We sat in the parking lot and ate our ice cream cones. She still wasn't saying too much to me, but I knew she was appreciative of the gesture. When I finished my cone, I pulled out of the parking lot and headed in the direction of my house. I would have taken Autumn home, but I knew she needed me right now. I was the only one that knew about her pregnancy, and in a way, I was glad of that. I didn't need her mama or sister all in her head trying to change up her thinking. I was sure that if they knew that she was pregnant, they would encourage her to keep it. It was better that they knew nothing about this whole situation and we keep it between the two of us. It was our child, so it was our business.

I pulled into my yard and killed the engine on my Camaro. I looked over at Autumn as she looked lonely out of the passenger window. She was lost in her thoughts, I knew that her mind must have been on overdrive. I exited the car and walked over to the passenger side of the car where she was sitting. I opened the door and kneeled down until I was eye level with her. I looked into her eyes as I placed her hand into mine. Her eyes were so full of hurt and pain, and I knew that I was the cause. I didn't have the words to make it better or to make the hurt go away. So I went with my first mind and kissed her. I pulled back and looked at her before kissing her again.

"I don't know what you are feeling Autumn, but I just want you to know that I am truly sorry for all of this. It was just the right thing to do at this time. You carried my child even if it was only a couple of weeks. Nobody else can say that they had that experience, that alone will always have us bonded."

Just hearing myself say it made it sink in, her and I really shared a child. We would be synced forever, and I honestly saw her in a different light right now. Like I started to care for her in a different light. She meant a little more to me now and that kind of scared me.

"I understand Deon, you were right I was just so hurt thinking on the what ifs. My mama would have killed me if she ever found out. I understand everything that you're saying. Like you said maybe if it was under different circumstances it would have been better," she said as she gave me a weak smile.

I held her hand as I pulled her out of the car. We walked into the house, and I locked the doors. She had a seat on the couch making herself comfortable as she started to watch TV. I wanted to do something nice for her knowing what she had just went through. I changed out of my good clothes and just put my robe on. I ran her a nice warm bubble bath. I went into the living room to grab her by her hand to lead her to the bathroom.

Once we were in there, I started to undress her, making sure to be extra careful with her. I didn't know if her body was in pain or not, but I didn't want to hurt her any more than I already had today. When she was completely naked, I helped her into the tub. I bathed her body from top to bottom. I was shocking myself with what I was doing right now. This wasn't me at all, but I didn't lie when I said I looked at her differently. A little part of me wished that I didn't make her get rid of the baby, but I guess everything happened for a reason. Maybe in another life.

After I was done bathing her, I helped her out of the tub and dried her off. I put lotion on her body and placed her in bed. I took me a nice hot shower then I went into the bedroom to join her. Taking my robe off I got in close to Autumn and spooned with her. I didn't even want to have sex I just wanted to be up under her taking in her scent. She smelled so good, and it felt good to have her in my arms. I held her all night as her tears wet up my arms. I just laid there, I knew that eventually, she would be okay. All I could think about was that I hope no one saw us together so that it wouldn't get back to Lani.

Chapter 15

KHELANI

Khalil definitely made my birthday one to remember. I was so happy about my brand-new car, and it was much needed. It was a little easier for JJ and me to maneuver around. Khalil never had us waiting or anything, but I knew that he couldn't always be two places at one time. I was so thankful for this man, over the course of a couple of months he has shown me just how hard he fucked with me. He was my better half, my best friend and there was no changing that. I was in it for the long ride. We were just good together.

His mom showing up was definitely something neither of us expected. I know that it was a big pill for Khalil to swallow, but I have seen a different side of him since she's been here. I've seen a more vulnerable side of him. At first, he had up this gigantic wall and was against the entire idea of hearing her out. He just wasn't feeling it at all. In a way, I could understand because someone showing up on your doorstep twenty-three years later claiming to be your mother will throw anyone off. We have talked numerous times about his childhood, and it wasn't anything pretty so her showing up could just have been a reminder of everything that he went through as a kid.

Khalil always told me that his parents didn't want him, that was how he ended up in foster care as an infant. That was just his logic not knowing the true reason his parents gave him up. I did my best to convince him to listen to what she had to say. Eventually, he softened up the more that I talked to him. I was glad that he did listen to me because he finally knew the truth and kind of got some background on his own story.

Just hearing the story about how evil her parents were to her made my heart ache for the both of them. That was something that you just didn't get over. That pain would always be with you. It was some cruel ass people in this world and to make your own child give up your flesh and blood was a different type of low. I could tell that she loved her child even though she never got the chance to raise him or know him.

The fact that she never stopped looking for her son really said a lot about her, she was genuine. I was just glad that she was here now and the both of them would have time to get acquainted with one another. She was so kind and down to earth. Her and I hit it off from the beginning. She loved the way that I loved her son, and she could see in his eyes just how much he loved me. I was talking to her like I had known her for years, but that's just how easy she was to talk to.

Being in her presence made me miss my mom so much. It had been years since the accident, but the pain was still fresh; I just had grown accustomed to hiding it. I always dealt with it when I was alone, not really wanting Khalil to worry about me or get JJ in his feelings about our parents. Connie was kind of feeling a void, and she had no clue. I didn't mind her living in the house with us at all.

Aretha has been in the nut house for a little while now, and I felt no remorse about it at all. That lady was so evil to us; she deserved everything that happened to her. She never really gave a fuck about us.

I was eighteen now, so that little check that she was getting was going to be cut off anyway. Just the thought of it made a wicked smile creep across my face. I wasn't an evil chick at all but when someone betrays me it was a must that you deal with the consequences, no matter who you were.

I hadn't heard from Autumn in a minute outside of school. I guess we both were just dealing with life right now. Connie showing up has taken all of Khalil and I attention. When I did see Autumn at school, she had a different vibe about her. I couldn't put my finger on it, but something was just off about her. She wasn't her normal jolly self, but whenever I would ask her, she would insist that she was fine. I didn't want to put any pressure on her to talk to me about whatever was bothering her, so I just let it be. When she was ready to talk I guess that she would let me know.

I was in the guidance office making sure everything was on track for me to graduate in May. My grades had significantly improved, and I was a straight A student. I was proud of myself because so many things happened my senior year, but I pressed through every obstacle. With the grades I had, I could easily get a scholarship to any school of my choice, but I wasn't really feeling the college thing right now. Maybe in the future but right now I had different plans for myself. As long as I got my diploma, I was good, that was all I was worried about. I wanted to show my little brother that education was important. He was on the right path, and I wanted to keep it that way. Even though I wasn't going to college, I still wanted that for him. JJ was a very intelligent young man, being on debate teams, and in different honor societies. I knew that our parents would be very proud of him. When the time comes, I would help him apply for multiple schools and scholarships. He was destined for greatness.

I was on the fence about going to prom or not. Simply because Khalil couldn't go with me, but I wouldn't mind going by myself. I would have to do some thinking on it. The bell rang, and it was now time to go home. I walked to my locker to put my books in and to grab my car keys. Once I had everything, I needed I headed out of the school to locate my car in the parking lot. I made it to my car and threw my backpack in the trunk. I sat in the car listening to music and texting Khalil as I waited for JJ.

He finally came out of the school carrying some girl's books as he walked her to her school bus. I just watched as he tried to get his mack on. The girl was cute, I could tell she was a nerd, but she was still a pretty girl. JJ was a nerd to he just didn't look like one. He walked her to the door of the bus like a gentleman and handed her books. They hugged, and he kissed her on her cheek before departing from her. He started jogging to my car, and I just smiled and shook my head.

I guess it had been a while since we had a sister and brother talk because it looked as if my baby brother had a little girlfriend.

"Jeremih I see you trying to get your little mack on, I see you boy!" I said as I pinched his jaws.

"Chill out Lani," he said laughing.

"She's pretty JJ, what's her name?"

"Her name is Destiny, we been talking for a little while now."

"Okay, that's what's up. You know you can talk

to me about anything right? Even sex."

"Laniiiii."

"I'm just saying, I know you're growing up and everything."

"I know Lani; but if I , I want to know of that nature I can talk to Lil about it."

"Okay, okay. I'm still your big sis though, don't forget that," I said feeling defeated.

I wasn't mad that he chose to talk to Khalil about it. I was glad that he had him to talk to. He was the big brother that JJ never had. I knew that it probably made him a little uncomfortable to talk to me about things of that nature, so Khalil was something like a saving grace. I knew he wouldn't tell him anything wrong.

When we arrived home, Connie and Khalil were sitting on the couch eating popcorn and watching TV. It was nice to see them getting along so well and enjoying one another's presence. I joined them while JJ went into his room to change clothes. After the movie went off, I went into the closet and grabbed a couple of board games and the Uno cards. We decided to turn the night into a game night. I was enjoying everyone, and Khalil and I was kicking ass as always. I looked around at all of their faces, and I felt a feeling of joy. I was blessed to have each and every one of them in my life.

The next day we woke up and ate breakfast together as a family. I decided that I would go to my senior prom after all. Autumn and I were going to go dress shopping today. Connie wanted to check out some Museums, so Khalil was going to take her. We all had our day planned out. I was a little excited about finding a dress now. I wanted it to be perfect, so I could look like a walking barbie doll. I was torn between a purple dress or a pretty blue color. Autumn wanted something green that would show off her melanin. Her skin was so pretty and dark as cocoa. A pretty green color dress would make her stand out, but I knew that whatever color she chose would look good on her. She was a gorgeous girl. Not like some people use the phrase 'she's pretty for a dark skin girl'. She was pretty anyway, dark skin, light skin didn't matter; we both were beautiful.

I went through to pick her up, and she was already standing outside waiting for me. She ended her call before getting into the car. We greeted one another with a hug as we sat in the car. I pulled off and proceeded to head around to different boutiques in search of the perfect dress for both of us. Our first couple of stops were a waste of time. It wasn't that their dresses weren't nice, they just weren't extravagant enough for me. It was my first and last prom, and I was trying to go out with a bang. This was a once in a lifetime opportunity, the only chance to go to prom was during your high school years.

Sure, someone who was still in school could invite you, but it still wouldn't be the same feeling of being a student yourself. I decided to go, so I was going to do it the right way. If Khalil could have went it would've made the experience better for me. I knew that if he was able to go, he would, but due to the age restrictions my man wasn't welcomed, and it was a bummer. Nevertheless, he encouraged me to go and get that experience because it was one he never got to have himself. If it wasn't for him encouraging me to do so, I wouldn't mind just being cuddled up with him on our couch as everyone else was at the prom.

I guess Autumn and I would be each other dates until after the prom was over. I already knew that I would be on the first thing smoking trying to make my way to Khalil. After going to two boutiques and looking at all of the dresses they had to offer I think we finally had a boutique that was worth our while. From the moment I walked into the store, I was in awe. The jewelry that was locked away in a see-through display immediately caught my attention. It was blinging from the sun hitting it through the window. Everyone knew that diamonds were a girl's best friend. They had a gold diamond choker that was to die for, and I knew I had to have it.

The woman that owned the store saw the jewelry catching my attention before I had a chance to pick out a dress. Just seeing the jewelry, I was almost sure that I would be able to find a dress to go with it. I found a purple dress that flip-flopped to pink in the light, a mermaid dress that was full of rhinestones and had a sweetheart neckline. I was in love with the dress, the rhinestones were gold with shimmer. I found some nice gold heels that were bedazzled to match the dress perfectly. It didn't take long at all to find everything that I needed. I was debating on getting a Tiara or not. I was already extra enough, so maybe that would have been taking it overboard, either way, I would still be looking like a queen. Crown or no crown, I was Khalil's queen, and he crowned me a long time ago.

Autumn found her a dress as well. She found her a lime green strapless dress that had a high split up the thigh that complimented her long legs. She went with some silver high heels that could have easily been stripper heels but still had just the right amount of class to them. We were set for prom, and now all we had to do was wait for the day to come. It was fun being out with Autumn, it had been a long time since we did anything like this. Just shopping and bonding like the old days and it felt good. She was talking more and seemed to be in a much better mood than she had been in lately. I was happy to see her smiling again even if I didn't know what the cause of her was not being in good spirits before. This was feeling like the old days as we went around the mall just buying little shit, just killing time. I had to have my cinnamon pretzel nuggets from Auntie Ann's, and she had her Cinnabun with caramel and pecans.

We sat in the food court eating and talking for a couple of hours just watching the people stroll by. We eventually grew tired of just sitting there, so we left the mall. Autumn and I headed to Khalil, and I crib to chill. The day was still young. When we arrived at the house no one was there so we did like we would normally do on a regular day. We sat on the porch, smoked and sipped on some wine coolers just to kill a little time until everybody got back home.

Autumn and I were still sitting on the porch laughing and talking. I was puffing on my black when Khalil's car pulled into the driveway. When he didn't get out immediately, I was a little thrown off until he texted me. He asked me to go ahead and take Autumn home, and I did as I was asked. I told her that Khalil and I had something to handle and that I would get up with her later. She didn't trip, and that was good because I honestly didn't feel like explaining anything to her. I wasn't even sure what was up myself.

I dropped Autumn off at home and headed back

to the house. I wasn't speeding, but I wasn't doing the speed limit either as I was trying to make it home to see what was up. My phone slid off of the leather seat to the side of the passenger seat. When I parked my car, I walked around to the passenger side to get my phone. As I was reaching under the seat to grab my phone, I noticed a pamphlet that fell on the side. Picking it up I noticed that it was a pamphlet to an abortion clinic. That really threw me for a loop. I knew for a fact that it wasn't mine. I cleaned my car out before Autumn, and I went shopping today, so no one had been in my car besides me and her . The pamphlet belonged to her, that was a given. I guess that explained why she had been acting so strange lately. She was pregnant, but she got rid of it, and I wondered why. I didn't even know that she was fuckin with someone that heavy. I guess shit between us was different now. She didn't even confide in me about it, I had no clue.

I knew that I hadn't been the best friend lately, but she played a part in us drifting apart as well. I was going to see just how long she would keep this secret from me. For now, I was going to see what was up with

SHE GOT IT BAD FOR A MONTGOMERY HITTA

my family.

Chapter 16

KHALIL

My mother had been asking me about some art museums here in the city. Imagine my surprise when I found out that she was a lover of the art as well. I guess we had more in common than I thought. That's why I had a love for art my mom was also fascinated, she adored some of the pieces I had in my place. I told her about the Montgomery Museum of Fine Arts. I had plans of taking there today, but it was unfortunate that I couldn't join her because I had to go check Hassan out on a business trip. Lani was out with Autumn doing some prom shopping. JJ had a math tournament out of the city, so it was no one else that was available to go with her. She assured me that she would be fine if I dropped her off and she would let me know when she was ready for me to come and get her. I was a little hesitant about it initially, but I finally agreed.

Hassan's crib was only a skip and hop from the museum so if she just so happened to need me I wouldn't be out of arms reach. Not that I was expecting anything bad to happen, just could never be too sure. Maybe it was just my way of thinking because of my training. Always expect the unexpected, that's the way I was taught. She was already dressed and waiting for me in the living room. Once I was dressed we headed out. We stopped at Zaxby's for a quick bite for lunch before heading to the museum.

"Alright ma, enjoy yourself. Hit my line if you need me and don't forget to let me know when you are ready," I said and then placed a kiss on her cheek.

"I will son," she said hugging me and kissing me on the cheek as well before exiting the car.

Over a short period of time, we have grown so close, and I had not one regret about it. We already had a mother and son bond, it was like it happened instantly. The fact that we had so much in common made it easy for us to bond. Like I like to tell Lani, I was her, just the male version. A newfound happiness has overtaken my life since she walked in. I was happy before with my life with Lani and JJ, they were my family before I ever knew that I had a living and breathing mother out here. It was just a new feeling to know where I came from, who I came from rather. Having a mother in my life was something I never really had a chance to experience as an orphan. I had it hard as hell growing up but to have her here right now meant the world to me. I don't know what the future holds but I would love for her to settle right here in Montgomery with Lani, JJ, and I. They've already grown very fond of her, and they enjoy having her around just as much as I do.

She talked to me about my pops, and I hate that he didn't have the chance to meet me and vice versa. Even with the life he lived, I could still tell that he was a very noble man, a lot like myself. Knowing how much he loved my mom made me feel something for him, even though I will never know him. I knew that if he would have lived, we probably would have been a big happy family, despite of what my sick ass grandparents had to say about it. They got just what they deserved though, and I feel no pity for them at all.

I headed over to Hassan's crib to kick shit with him for a little while and to see what was cracking on the business tip. When I walked into his man cave where he was shooting pool, his son JP was walking out. It had been a while since I had seen him. I guess he has been handling his business and staying out of the way. That was the best way to be in my opinion.

"What's up man?" I said dapping him up with a brotherly hug.

"What's crackin bro? I don't mean to run out on you, I just have a play to handle right quick," he said.

"I feel you, bro. Do your thing."

"That boy is out here doing everything that he's saying he's not. I've tried my best to raise him up the right way, so he doesn't turn to the streets as a youngin' the same way that I did," Hassan said to me.

"All you can do is tell him what's good for him. It's up to him to follow the correct path. He's a smart dude, he'll be straight."

"I hope you're right young blood. I just feel like he's keeping something from me, I just can't put my finger on it. I'll let it be for now," he said as he shot the eight ball into the corner pocket.

We chopped it up for about an hour. Just talking about where Lani was with her training and everything. He didn't have any hits lined up for me, so that was good news for me. That meant I would be able to spend more quality time with my family. When I got back in my car, I noticed that my mom left her cell phone on the seat. It had only been a little under an hour since I dropped her off. She probably wasn't ready to go just yet, so I would just drop the phone off to her. I made it to the museum in no time. I had nothing else to do so I decided I would just join her and check out some art. Maybe I would get some new pieces to go into my apartment.

I grabbed her phone and exited the car. Just walking into the museum, I was in awe at all of the fascinating pieces that adorned the wall of the museum. I had to break my attention from the art and started looking around for my mom. I hadn't spotted her yet, and that was a little strange. I noticed a young lady who was walking around with a name tag, so I assumed she worked here. I asked her if she saw a woman who fit my mother's description. She informed me that she saw her walking towards the back and I thanked her. I walked towards the way that she saw her. As soon as I turned the corner, I saw a bald bulky man pulling her towards the emergency exit of the building. When I finally made it to the door, he pulled off in a F-150 pickup truck. I knew then that that was the man that she had been running from all of this time. The audacity of this nigga to follow her here on some fuck shit. As long as breath was in my body, he wasn't going to get away with this. She wasn't going back with that nigga even if my life depended on it.

Running back to the front of the museum to exit out, I was running full speed. I was trying to get to my car as quickly as I could. When I finally made it to my car I started it up and pulled out as fast as I could to catch up with them. I put the car into sports mode pushing the car to get that extra turbo speed. I finally saw him, and he was two cars ahead. I trailed him all the way to an abandoned road, and it was a dead end. The truck was swerving left and right, and I could see through the back window how he was constantly hitting her and throwing her head against the window. My blood pressure was through the fuckin roof. It was taking everything in me not to shoot the tires off of that damn truck. If I didn't fear for my mother's life, I would have. I just prayed that he didn't try to kill her before I had a chance to rescue her. When I get my hands on that nigga, I was going to do him dirty, and he would know that he was fuckin with the wrong family.

He was approaching the dead end of the road, and the truck came to a shrieking halt. I didn't give a fuck if he knew I was following them. There was no way I was letting him take my mama from me again, no one was going to come in between us again. We were just having the chance to be a family, and I just couldn't let that slip through my grasp. This shit wasn't happening to me again. At this moment I just didn't give a fuck about nothing, I was on straight fuckin savage mode. I had officially lost it. I hopped out of the car with my gun already aimed. He quickly made his way around and pulled her up into a choke hold with a gun to her head.

"I don't know who the fuck you are playboy, but your best bet is to mind your own business."

"I ain't your fuckin playboy homie! You got the game all fucked up, now your best fuckin bet is to let her go before I place a bullet in your dome. And trust me that's not a fucking threat, and I'll have you to know I make well on all my damn promises. So, try me if you want to."

"It's funny that you think that I would be intimidated by a little pretty boy like you. You don't put any fear in my heart bitch boy," he said.

My muscles in my jaw tightened like they always did whenever I got mad. My chest started to heave up and down. He was testing my gangsta right now, and it was fucking with me. For a minute I stood there with my gun aimed at him, and he had his gun to her head. I knew what I had to do. I just feared for her life in the process. This shit was like something straight out of a movie. I have never been afraid to kill before, but right now I was scared shitless. Not for my life but for my mothers. Something was telling me that this nigga wouldn't hesitate on pulling the trigger and I knew that it would end her life instantly. I toyed back and forth with the idea on how I wanted to handle the situation. Just to see then dried up tears on her face. Her face swollen from him repeatedly hitting her in the face. To hear her begging for her life made me hurt and realize just what she had been experiencing with this nigga for the longest.

At that moment I knew just what the fuck I had to do. There was no longer a question about it. The fuck nigga had to go. For all the pain and heartbreak that he took my mom's through he would pay for that shit with his life. I saw him starting to squeeze the trigger and sent a shot straight to his head dropping him instantly. My mother cried hysterically as his blood splattered into her face. I should have done it a long time ago but just as I expected that nigga would have killed her. I wasn't going to give him the opportunity to do that shit though. It was either her life or his, and it was no questioning about who had to go. I could see the hurt written all over her face as I ran to her and held her in my arms. We stood there and hugged for what felt like an eternity as I let her get all of her emotions out.

I knew that she was probably a little traumatized and full of emotion right now, but we had to do something with this body and this truck. The both of them had to be disposed of. I placed his body into the truck and set it on fire. We left the scene without a trace. I took my mother back to the crib, so she could gather her thoughts and get cleaned up. When I pulled up Autumn and Lani were sitting on the porch. Not wanting Autumn's nosey ass all in our business I texted Lani and told her to go ahead and drop her off at home. When they pulled out of the driveway, we exited the car and walked into the house. My mom continued to thank me over and over again for saving her life. I had to let her know that as her son I would always have her back. She got in the shower, and I did the same in the room Lani, and I shared.

Once I was done taking my shower, I went to burn our clothes. Lani was in the room waiting on me to see what happened. I gave her the full rundown on everything that happened tonight. She checked on me, but her first instinct was to go check on my mother. We both went into the room where my mother was sleeping. When we walked in the room, she was just laying down in the bed looking at the wall as tears rolled down her face.

Lani sat on the bed beside her and just started rubbing her back. I didn't have the words to help ease whatever pain she was feeling. I was just glad that she was still here with us. I was sure that at one point she may have loved the guy, but over the years a person will make you hate them. His actions toward her made her see him in a different light. He was nothing but a possessive man who wanted to control every fiber of her being.

"I don't want y'all to confuse my tears with tears of sadness. They are really tears of joy and happiness. I'm just thankful to be rid of that bastard. He had put me through so much over these last couple of years to the point it was draining, and I was severely depressed. The crazy ass man had a tracker on my phone, that's how he knew I was in Montgomery. He told me that he had been following me for some while now. That shit was crazy as hell because not once did I think he would run up on me at a damn museum.

He was determined to find me and bring me back home, but there was no way I was going back to that life or him. If I would've went back, I knew that I would have ended up dead ,. When I got here and only when I got here did I start to feel like myself again. I'm just thankful for you son and all that you have done for me since I just popped into your life. You as well Lani, y'all welcomed me with open arms and have shown me nothing but unconditional love and for that, I'm forever grateful," my mom said to Lani and I.

"We got your back ma; I'm just glad that you no longer have to worry about that man. He'll never be able to hurt you again. I'm here for whatever you need don't hesitate to reach out for anything."

"I know baby, I love the both of you."

"We love you too ma," I said to her as I held her hands.

We stayed in the room with her just, so she could be around us and not have to be alone. Lani showed ma her prom dress and everything that she bought for her senior prom. That got my mother's mind off of tonight's activities momentarily. I was just glad that it did for the time being because I didn't like seeing her that way. She was loving Lani's dress just as much as she was. I loved it as well, and I couldn't wait to see my queen in it. I knew that she would be as beautiful as she was on her birthday if not more beautiful.

I was so happy that I encouraged her to go. Just talking about it made her eyes light up. I just didn't feel like it would be right for her not to attend her senior prom. Those memories were ones that she would be able to look back on in the future and be able to smile about. Something that she would be able to reminisce on. I hate that I couldn't go because of age restrictions, but I would still play a part in her day to make it special for her. I already had plans underway that she had no clue about. I had to go pick up my tux next week, and she was going to flip out when she sees me in it. Even though I can't go to prom with her, I wanted to surprise her after prom dressed in my tux. I would be on my suave shit that night and treat her just the way that a true gentleman would. I wanted her to end her night on a good tip, and I knew just the sight of me would bring her so much happiness. I'd do anything to keep a smile on my baby's face.

When ma finally fell asleep Lani, and I creeped out of her room. As we were walking out JJ was entering the house. He told us that they won first place in the math competition and we congratulated him on that. JJ was a smart guy, and I was glad that he was on the right path. It was so many young guys his age that were out here in the streets involved in all kind of gang related activities. For that, I was proud of him because in this city there were so many things to get into that was negative, but he stayed clear of all of that. It was so easy to become a statistic out here and become a product of your environment, but that wasn't the case with him. He never let the hype of being able to hang out and do street shit persuade him to be on the same thing. He had his own mine and moved differently than some of his peers.

Lani and I gave him freedom because we trusted that he knew right and wrong. We didn't have to worry about him getting himself into no shit. He was just a real standup guy, and I was honored to be the big brother that he looked up to. Recently he has come to me to talk about this girl that he had been dating. I could tell that he really liked the girl by the way he spoke so highly of her. From my understanding, they had a lot in common, and that was always a good thing. I gave him the talk about the birds and bees per say to let him know that I was once his age and I know how the urges come. Letting him know that he didn't have to necessarily be in a rush but if he felt like he was ready, I encouraged him to protect himself.

I told him to watch out for certain kind of females. Especially the bird hoes that was out to get a good nigga. He had a lot going for himself, and some girls preyed on a guy like that. I was putting him up on game so that he wouldn't become a victim of that shit. I wasn't a pro or anything, but I could hip him to everything that I know. He appreciated everything that I told him, and I let him know that any time he needed to talk that I was here for him.

Lani and I finally made our way to our room. I sat between her legs as she started to massage my shoulders. I was tense as hell, and it was definitely needed. Her soft hands felt so good against my skin. Her massage was putting my mind at ease. I just wanted to be up under her right now. Lani had a way of calming me down and making everything that bothered me mysteriously disappear. She was my saving grace. The woman was just everything a nigga like me ever needed.

I never looked for it, but I have always known what type of woman I wanted to be with when I decided to settle down. When I met her, there was no question if she was the wifey type or not. She was made for me, and I was made for her. That was evident in the way that we always came to each other's beck and call.

That shit with ol dude and my mom was crazy as hell, and I had a feeling that this wasn't the end of all of the crazy shit. I was the type of nigga to cross bridges when I got to them. As of right now, I don't think there were any more pressing matters that required my attention. So hopefully I could just chill for a while and get my head back on straight.

I woke up the next day feeling a lot better

than the night before. My mom was in a much better mood, and that made my day so much better. I had a quick four-hour shift today at Foot Locker, so I was getting ready for work. Since I wasn't going to be at work long today, I insisted that Lani just chill in the house with my mom until I got back. Even though she assured me that she was straight now, I just didn't want her to be alone. Being alone sometimes forced you to think about all of the bullshit you try to keep your mind off of. You would be sitting around overthinking for no reason. I know because I've been there numerous of times.

It was a rainy Saturday anyway, so it wasn't much to do but stay in the house and relax. They would probably watch a couple of movies and sleep. That was normally what we did in my household when it rained. I was glad that I wouldn't have to be away from them for too long. I was going to knock out these little few hours and head straight back home to cuddle up with my woman. This rainy weather always made us feel some type of way, and I could never turn down any good loving from my lady.

I arrived at work thirty minutes later and clocked in on the computer screen. It was a pretty slow day because the rain had everyone cooped in the house. I wasn't tripping at all, it was some little easy cash. Nine times out of ten I would give the check to Lani for gas or to get her nails and shit done. I was playing iMessage game against Lani when I heard the bell on the door chime, indicating that someone had entered the store. I looked up and saw JP. I walked up to him, and we kicked shit in the store for a while. We were catching up so long he forgot what he came in the store for. He copped some 12's and the shirt to match.

From my point of view, it seems as if he was on the straight and narrow. I couldn't see what Hassan was speaking on previously, but I wasn't the one to pry. I couldn't just be in the man's business. If there was something he wanted me to know he knew how to reach me. JP and I had a relationship because his father was the only father figure I've ever known. When Hassan took me in JP sort of became like a little brother to me. As he started growing up, I wasn't able to be around so much because my occupation didn't permit me to do so. Nevertheless, the love for him was still the same, that bond would always be there.

Once he paid for his items, he promised that we would start getting up more and not let so much time go by before we see one another again. Catching up with him gave me a good feeling, and I was glad that we had the opportunity to do so. There were a couple of shoe stores in the city, but he chose the Foot Locker I was working at. That let me know that he didn't want to run out the other day for real he just had something to do. I respected that. It would make Hassan feel a little at ease to know that we spoke and caught up today. I knew he was worried about his son because that's all he could really talk about the last time I saw him.

My little four hours sped by quickly after JP left the store. I was glad because it was still raining and all I wanted was to be home. I was blessed for that short shift, it was perfect timing with the rain. Most people hated the rain but since I've had someone to spend my days with I've grown to love them. It gave me an excuse to be lazy and watch TV all day with my better half. I was stopping at the store to get all of us some ice cream and snacks for the weather. I stopped by the red box on the way home to pick up a couple of movies, and we were set.

I went into the bathroom to take a quick shower before joining Lani in the bed. She wasted no time pressing play on the movie. We sat with our backs against the headboard sharing a box of Cookies and Cream ice cream. Moments like this with her were priceless, and I appreciated every precious second that we spent together.

Lani and I watched three movies together before we grew tired of looking at the TV. We just laid in bed and pillow talked. She was going on and on about the prom. The theme was recently changed to Masquerade, and that had her all hyped up. She had no clue about all of the things that I had in store for her prom night. I couldn't wait to see her face when she sees what will be waiting for her. I succeeded with making her eighteenth birthday one to remember. She was in love with her brand-new car. She never told me that it was her dream car. When I saw it on the Nissan lot, it instantly reminded me of her. The car had Lani's name written all over it, so I went into the dealership and copped it for her with no hesitation. After being with her these couple of months, we have learned one another. I knew just what she liked and vice versa. These months easily felt like years with her.

The day that we met, I would have never known that she would be so important to me today. Life was funny that way, but I am grateful that the man above and the universe saw fit for us to be an item. My Lani, my Lani, I thought to myself.

Chapter 11

DEON

Shit between Autumn and I had been crazy. Not even in a bad way though. I was starting to feel shit for her that I never intended to intentionally. It is so crazy that her being pregnant with my child for that short period of time changed my whole outlook on her. I was looking at shit in a whole different light now. I cared about her a little more now, and I honestly didn't know how to handle that shit. It fucked with my head on whole 'nother level. It was like a part of me wanted to back out of this shit that we had going because I was scared of how it would go. I wasn't even supposed to be feeling like this about this bitch, but here I was.

I couldn't even focus on that shit Lani had going on because Autumn and I was now to the point of no return. We were in this shit too deep, there was no turning back at this point. The crazy part about the whole situation was that we had been on this creeping shit for months now and Lani still didn't know about it. It wasn't on me anymore to put the shit out there. That shit was on Autumn after all, Lani was her best friend, not mines. Technically I didn't owe her shit, and no longer gave a fuck about the whole ordeal. At the same time, all I could think about in the back of my head is when my old head would say the saying 'what's done in the dark will come to the light'. I normally didn't believe in all of that superstitious shit, but lately I just had the feeling that the shit could have some truth to it. I can't even explain the shit, but I just felt like it is what it is.

Autumn and I have been up under so much lately it didn't feel right when we weren't in each other's presence. One thing for certain though was that my grind never stopped, and she was still in school. Lately, I had been thinking about relocating and setting up shop in a new city. I don't know I just needed a change of scenery in my life. I was sick of looking at the same ol shit, dealing with the same ol stupid motherfuckers on the daily. All of this shit was just getting pretty old to me. It had been a little while since I had done anything for myself. I hadn't had a chance to do any shopping lately because I been in the streets grinding. I had been through the mall to scoop a couple of fits. I just needed some shoes to go with each of them. I could have gotten them in the mall, but it was getting packed in there, and I didn't too much fuck with a crowd.

I stopped at a couple of stores in the city picking up shoes. Every store I went into was out of the new J's that dropped today, and it was only one more spot to hit up. I made my way over to Fairview to see if Hibbet Sports had the kicks I was looking for. Imagine my surprise when I was turning into the parking lot, and I saw that nigga JP walking out of the store. At that moment I forgot all about the damn shoes. I had been checking for this nigga for weeks, and he hadn't turned up until now. He was going to wish that he stayed his ass in hiding just a little while longer. I was feeling like I just hit the jackpot or something. I couldn't even think about exactly how I wanted to murk this nigga, but all I knew was that the nigga had to be got.

I stalled for a minute trying not to let him see

me. He was oblivious to me in the duck off parked. I watched as he entered his car and pulled off. I followed behind him as he maneuvered through the city. About twenty minutes later he pulled up to an abandoned house which I assumed was a trap house. As soon as he was getting out of the car, I put my piece off safety and riddled his body with bullets and sped the fuck off. I was just glad that shit was done. I knew the nigga was dead because I let off nothing but head and chest shots. There was no need to get out and check because I already knew what my gunplay was about. I had a good mind to go back and get the shoes but I just said fuck it, I already had enough anyway.

I didn't see anyone out on the streets when I killed dude, so I wasn't too much worried about shit. Now that he was out the picture and I didn't have anyone else out here fucking with my money I felt ten times better about a lot of shit. The shit was so crazy because JP had been fucking with me for a while now and the shit had to come down to that. It was on his ass though because he just was out here roaming the streets like he didn't have a debt owed to me. He knew exactly what he was getting into when he stepped foot in this game. Shit like that was bound to happen if you moved the wrong way and crossed a nigga like me. Nobody was out here letting motherfuckers fuck them over. If I would have continued to let him slide, then that would only give these other niggas the motive that they could try me on the same bullshit. I wasn't going for that, fuck nah!

I didn't know too much about the nigga besides the fact that he was slanging for me. We were close in age, but I still looked at him as a little nigga under me. I never really heard him talk too much about family, so I assumed he didn't have much family. In my mind, I was feeling like no one would even miss his ass off of the streets. I went home and kicked my feet up as I smoked a couple of blunts to ease my mind. The way that shit went down I knew that someone probably had found his body by now and it would be on the news before the day was over with. I was just sitting back waiting for the shit to unfold.

I heard a knock on the door, and for a minute I just sat there and pretended not to be home, not really being in the mood for company right now. I continued to blow o's out of my mouth when my phone dinged indicating that I had a text message. Opening up the message it was from Autumn telling me to unlock the door, she was outside. Against my better judgment I got up from where I was sitting and opened the door for her. She looked nice as hell when she walked in, and I could tell she had just got done getting her hair done for the prom. Shorty was looking right and just looking at her pretty smooth chocolate skin made my dick rock up, getting harder and harder by the second. I moved to the side letting her in the house as I continued to smoke.

She hugged me really tight, and I hugged her back. She smelled so good as I inhaled her scent. She had her prom dress in her hand and was showing it off to me. It was a different kind of glow about her, I could tell that she was genuinely happy today. That made me happy to see that she was in much better spirits. Since the whole abortion thing, she was kind of down and out about the whole ordeal. I have been by her side a little more since that went down. It made our bond grow stronger. She kind of wanted me to escort her to the prom, but I couldn't risk that. She shouldn't want to risk it herself. I guess her ass was feeling real reckless, but I wasn't with that shit. Shit was straight how it was now, and I wanted to keep it this way until I figured out how I wanted to move with this situation. To make her feel better, I promised to get us a hotel room tonight, and she could just meet me there when the prom after party was over. That made her ease up off me a little bit, for now anyway.

We chilled at the house for a while until it was time for her to head home and get ready for the prom. I dropped her off at her crib and just rode around the city for a while. I slid through the hood to check on my mama and little sister to see how they was doing. I haven't had a chance to spend some quality time with them, and I had a little down time right now, so that's what I decided to do. I don't know why I just had the urge to show my face. My mama was always calling to check on me and to see how I was doing. I had been ripping and running the street so much I didn't make as much time for them like I used to.

When I walked into the house the smell of soul food filled my nostrils, and my stomach instantly started to growl.

"Ma?" I yelled as I followed the smell into the kitchen.

"In here baby," she said to me.

I entered the kitchen, and my mom was standing at the stove with her apron on whipping up a good meal. I was right on time. I pulled up a seat at the kitchen table as she continued to cook.

"Dinner will be done in a minute baby, I hope that you will be joining your sister and me."

"Yeah ma, I can stay I don't have anywhere. I need to be right now."

She turned the stove eyes off and rubbed her hands on her apron before pulling out a seat to join me at the table. Her face wore a look of seriousness, and I already knew what direction this conversation was heading towards. She just looked in my face for a while, and I could see the hurt all over her face as tears welled up in her eyes. This was one of the reasons I didn't come around as often because she would get in her feelings about me being in the streets. When I started slanging that was our only means for survival. It was only so much my mom could do as a single parent. I hated seeing her struggle to provide for me and my sister.

What type of nigga would I be to sit there and watch my mama struggle to provide? I did the only thing a hood nigga knew to do in this situation. I started hugging the block relentlessly. My mama never respected what I did, but she appreciated the gesture in a way. I was doing enough to keep our heads above water, and for that little bit, she was grateful. She didn't like the fact that I dropped out of school and let go of my football scholarship. Eventually, she knew there wasn't much anyone could tell me once my mind was made up. I was a man at the age of sixteen, I became the man of the house for real then, and you couldn't tell me otherwise. I never got out of line with my OG, that wasn't in me, but in my head, I was grown. I was paying bills, buying groceries for the house, and all of the household necessities. We weren't wanting for shit at that point.

My mama worked by choice. Reluctantly she accepted money from me, but she put it all into a savings account, and she has been good ever since. Which was, even more, a reason she saw fit for me to get out of the game. I honestly didn't see myself doing so anytime soon. She feared that I would lose my life to the streets the same way that my father did when I was a kid. That was her biggest problem with me being in the streets and the fact that I could be using my God given talent to make an honest living.

I had been doing this so long, and I just couldn't see myself going back to my old life playing football. Don't get me wrong, I still loved the sport til this day. That just wasn't a part of me anymore. I was a street nigga in every sense of the word, and there was no changing that at this point.

"Dee baby, you don't know how much I worry about your well-being on the daily. Scared that I'm going to get that call that something bad has happened to you son. I don't want the same thing that happened to your father to happen to you, Deon. I can't bare that type of heartache baby. You and your sister are all I have left in this lonely world. I just pray that one day soon you let this life go before it takes you away from me," she said as tears began to slowly run down her face.

I hated to see her this way. I never liked to see my mama shed a single tear. To know that I was the cause of her tears really was fucking with my head. Looking at her like this made tears well up in my eyes. I wouldn't dare let a tear fall though. For some odd reason, I felt that it made me less of man. I don't know why but I just felt that way.

"Ma you don't have to worry about me out here, I'm straight," I tried my best to assure her.

My little sister walked into the kitchen and ma wiped the tears from her face quickly.

"Hey baby, dinner is ready. Go get washed up and come join us."

She did as she was told and came back to have a seat by her big brother. I guess she missed me, I missed my little sis too. I made a promise to myself that from this day forward that I would make more time for my two main ladies. They deserved that from me and so much more. For now, I would just take baby steps towards it.

My mama had prepared a feast on this good Saturday like today was Sunday or something. I guess she was just in the mood to cook a big meal. Either way, I wasn't complaining, and I was glad that I stopped by. She prepared collard greens with neckbones and hamhocks in them, buttermilk cornbread, fried chicken, homemade mac and cheese, and candied yams. She fixed a nigga a big boy plate, and I was ready to dig in. As soon as I picked up my fork and placed it in the greens, she smacked my hand. I was too busy being greedy that I forgot all about saying grace. I should have known she would make us say it. We held hands, bowed our heads, and closed our eyes as my mama said the prayer.

Once she was finished praying, we all dug into our plates. It had been a minute since I had a good home cooked meal from my mama. Made me miss the hell out of her cooking because my mama could throw down in the kitchen. I would have to make it my business to stop by and get some of her cooking. When we were finished eating, I sat with them for a little while. It was a good feeling to be around the two women who mean the most to me. They were my purpose for living. My mom and sister were really my everything in a nutshell.

Autumn was blowing my phone up with pictures of her in her prom dress and shit. I must admit she was looking good as hell. As I looked over the pictures that she sent to me. I felt a hint of jealousy take over my body as I imagined all of the niggas that would be checking her out tonight. She begged me to stop by and see her before she left, and I obliged. I was a little reluctant at first, not wanting to run into Lani. She assured me that I wouldn't, so I slid through. When I pulled up her mom and sister were snapping pics of her. I watched on before getting out. This was kind of weird to me because I've never really been around her people. They greeted me, but I could feel a little negative vibe from her mother. I brushed it off not wanting to fuck up Autumn's day. I just smiled and continued to be courteous for her sake.

Her sister Shaunie insisted that we take a picture

together. I could tell that Autumn wanted to, so I did. Lani called her to let her know that she was on her way and that was my cue to get the fuck out of dodge. I headed over to the Doubletree downtown to book our room for the night. I was going to get us a nice cozy suite. As soon as I stepped foot into the lobby of the hotel, the clerk was being overly friendly. I just grinned to myself. All I could think about was that Boosie song when he said, 'all these hoes love rappers and hood niggas.' He didn't lie about that shit at all. Sack chasing hoes, I thought to myself. She slid me the room card on the counter along with a card with her number on it. I picked up the room key and left the card sitting there.

"I'm smooth shorty," letting her know that I wasn't interested. She gave me a look of disgust, but I could give zero fucks. I didn't have time for the fuck shit today. I went into our room and just kicked back and chilled until Autumn was done with the prom.

Chapter 18

KHELANI

The day that I had been waiting for since I was a

little girl had finally come. I was ecstatic because it was a reminder of two things. One that the school year was coming to an end and most importantly that I would be walking across that stage in no time. I never expected my senior year to roll around as quickly as it did, but I'm not complaining because it was just time for me to face the real world and see it for the fucked up cold world that it was. I already knew this because in many ways I already had experienced the worst of it. Practically having to raise my baby brother while still being a child myself, I was forced to be an adult. Even though back then I didn't participate in all things that grownups did I still felt older than I was. I couldn't focus on that though, JJ was young, and he needed me. I had to suck up that sucker shit and put my big girl panties on and become the big sister he needed me to be. We only had one another, so it was only right. I'm sure that my parents wouldn't have had it any other way.

Sometimes it saddened me to know that my parents would not be able to see me walk across that stage, but I knew that they would be there in spirit.

That alone was enough to make me smile. I was so ready to hit this prom tonight with my bestie. We were going to be two of the baddest bitch's JD ever saw on prom night. If we weren't the only two bad bitches, no cocky shit just speaking facts. These broads our age was basic as hell, and half of them had no clue what fashion was. I always dressed to impress no matter the occasion. But since there was an occasion tonight, it was a given that I was going to come through and shut down the whole scene. My baby wouldn't be there, but that was okay because his presence would have brought me so many jealous stares. That's how the females were in this city. They didn't have to have a reason to hate; that's just how they were.

"Okay just a few more baby, you look so beautiful Lani," mama Connie said to me.

She was giving me a full-blown photo shoot. Her, Khalil, and JJ had me feeling like a black Cinderella right about now. I was feeling absolutely beautiful, and Khalil was constantly reminding me. My gown complimented my thick frame. It looked as if it was painted on me, but I was comfortable. I wore a 360

Brazilian lace frontal that was wand curled to perfection. I had my makeup done professionally, and my face was beat to the gawds! I was ready for this prom now. I knew that I was looking good and that made me feel good. I had waited so long for this day to come just to get dressed for the occasion. This was my first prom, so I was excited to see what it would be like. Just to see what the atmosphere would be like. I was in a mood for a good time and good vibes with my classmates. I didn't normally fuck with my class, but tonight I was going to vibe with everyone. That was how good of a mood I was in.

After taking all of the pictures we could possibly take Khalil walked me to my car and I proceeded to leave so that I could pick Autumn up for the prom. Neither of us had dates, so we were going to thug it out together as best friends. When we pulled up at the venue the parking lot was already overflowing with cars. We were already pumped seeing everyone heading to the entrance of the building. I found a decent parking spot where we didn't have to walk too far to get to the door. Once I parked we freshened up with our perfume, checked our faces in the mirror, grabbed our clutches and exited the car.

My best friend and I was looking bad as hell, and that was evident by the stares we got from the niggas and the looks of envy we got from the females. I held my dress up to keep it from touching the ground. The music was beating as we entered into the ballroom. People were already on the dance floor getting their party on. There were so many smiling faces in the building I couldn't help but smile myself. This was one hell of a year, and we was near the finish line. That was definitely something to party about. I was a little parched, so we headed over to the table where the refreshments were. I grabbed me a little cup and filled it up with the homemade punch. Autumn was munching on chicken tenders and fruit. We were laughing and talking with a couple of our classmates.

Looking at the time on my phone I noticed that it was time for us to take our prom pictures. We headed in the direction where the pictures were being taken and stood in line until the photographer was ready for us. I was going to take my individual pictures first before Autumn, and I had a picture together. I held my mask to my eyes and smiled for the pictures. I was taking a lot of pictures because I wanted something to choose from. Autumn took her individual pictures, and my best friend looked so beautiful. I don't know what it was, but she had a glow about herself, and it was more than her makeup highlight popping. She looked genuinely happy, and it warmed my heart to see her this way. Once the pictures were done, we made our way to the dance floor and started ripping it up. We were killing shit in typical Autumn and Lani fashion. We were having such a good time, and it was the most fun we had in a long time.

We were doing everything from the cha-cha slide to the wobble. I loved me a good ol line dance, especially when everyone knew how to do it. We were having so much fun. I could only imagine what graduation night would be like. I know that it is going to be lit. Prom was finally coming to an end, and I didn't want it to be over, but there were hella after parties taking place tonight, so I would find out which one was going to jump then maybe Khalil and I could swing through. My phone dinged, and I looked down, and it was a text from my better half asking me to meet him out front. Autumn and I headed towards the exit as everyone else was leaving.

I walked down the stairs looking down as I held my dress up so that it wouldn't touch the ground. I looked up and looked directly into the eyes of Khalil dressed in a black tuxedo looking as handsome as ever. He was standing in front of a horse and carriage; the horses were snow white, and so was the carriage. The carriage had pink and white flowers adorning it. It was so beautiful; the sight was amazing, and Khalil really had outdone himself this time. I walked to him slowly as he met me half way. I felt so loved at this moment, he knew how to make me feel special. He couldn't be with me at prom, but he knew he had to do something to make up for the little lost time. That was just the type of man that Khalil was, and I loved him for that. I was hearing so many "aww's" from people looking on and walking by, and that made me blush even harder. Autumn was also egging us on and looking happy for us. I asked her if she could drive my car home and we would be by to get it later. She said that she would just drop it off at our house and catch her a ride to wherever she was going.

That was all we needed to hear, I handed her the keys, and she was on her merry little way. Khalil held my hand and helped me into the carriage and then got inside himself. He handed me a single rose, and I put it to my nose and started to sniff it with a smile on my face. The rose was so beautiful, and it was a meaningful gesture.

"Khalil it's beautiful, all of this is beautiful baby. You've outdone yourself this time. I don't think anything that you have done can top this moment. This is almost as good as my birthday," I said to him playfully.

"Anything for my number one lady and trust me, baby, I have many tricks up my sleeve to keep you smiling. I shocked myself at times with the things I think of," he said and we started to laugh.

He instructed the driver that he could pull off, and we did slowly. It was a nice out, not too hot or too cold. The breeze that was out felt just right to my skin. I cuddled up close to Khalil, and he turned and placed a soft kiss on my forehead. I closed my eyes and blushed, as my heart fluttered from the touch of his lips. He stroked my face lightly. The carriage ride was nice and pleasant, my day had been made already and the night was still young. We rode around the city in the carriage for about thirty minutes.

As our ride was coming to an end Khalil's phone started to ring and normally at a time like this he wouldn't have answered but seeing that it was Hassan he picked up immediately. This was a very inopportune time, so I knew something had to be up. Just by the look on Khalil's face, I knew exactly what time it was. He listened intently to whatever Hassan was saying before he spoke. Khalil jaw muscles started to tighten, and I knew that what was being said on the other end of the phone had pissed him off in just that instant.

"You want me to ride on this nigga right now?..bet," was all he said before he ended his call. He asked the drive to take him to his car.

"Baby I hate to end the night this way, I wanted

you to enjoy your night. I had no intentions for anything like this to pop off today out of all days. Fuck man!" he said madly as he held his head in his hands.

"Bae, what's wrong? talk to me," I said as I placed both of my hands on his shoulders and leaned on his back.

A lone tear escaped his eyes, and I was scared to hear what his response would be. The only other time I has seen him shed a tear was when he was meeting his mom for the first time. We were having such a good night and one phone call killed the mood. I knew that it wasn't Khalil's fault, but I still wanted to know what was up.

"JP is dead Lani, they found him unresponsive lying beside his car in the hood. The shit is fucked up on so many levels Lani. I just saw bruh the other day at the store, he was trying to leave all this shit behind and be the nigga his daddy wanted him to be. His dad had suspicions that he was living like this and he was really worried about him. Just when a nigga decides to turn his life around. That was life for your ass though, every time a nigga tries to do the right thing shit like this happens. The shit you never really see coming. This one is fuckin with me bae."

"I'm sorry about that baby, I really am. I know that he was like a little brother to you, but baby one thing I know is that God's timing is never wrong. Sometimes we don't understand why things happen the way they do, and we may never know. One thing I had to learn was the only thing we need to understand is that everything isn't meant to be understood," I said to him.

The driver had arrived back at Khalil's car, and we exited the carriage. He paid the driver and we got into his car and sped off.

"I heard everything that you said back there baby, and you are right. I just can't wrap my head around this shit right now. Hassan wants me to ride on the nigga that did the shit tonight."

"Does he know who did it?"

"He doesn't, but quite frankly I don't give a fuck because he was about to meet the grim reaper. You riding or not? This is the moment of truth ma."

"I'm riding with you bae, right or wrong."

"That's all I need to know ma," he said as he grabbed my hand and our fingers interlocked.

We were still dressed elegant as hell, but at this moment right now neither of us gave a fuck. Khalil had the whereabouts of the nigga that murked JP, and we were on the way to see about this nigga. Money man was blaring through the speakers as he handed me the glocks to load them up. This was the moment of truth for real just as Khalil said. He was driving, and I was getting shit ready. Luckily the bottom of my dress was detachable, so I took it off and threw it in the backseat. Khalil was out of his tuxedo jacket and only had his button up on. I can't believe we was about to do this shit in formal attire, but it was what the fuck it was. When it was time to ride, it was time to ride, and there were no questions that needed to be asked. I was his down bitch, and he didn't have to doubt that.

At this moment right now, I felt that Bryson Tiller song ' Set It Off' was perfect for the occasion even though it was R&B. It was Khalil's and I song, and it described the type of rider I was for him. When I said that I meant that shit with every fiber of my being. I had been preparing for this shit for a long time, and I was trained to motherfuckin go!

She just might be the one for me

Ain't no need to question, now, bitch

She 'a pull the gun for me

Pop two, she 'a take one for me

Set it off, if a bitch come for me

Set if off, if a nigga come for me

She 'a pull the gun for me

Pop two, she 'a take one for me

Set it off, if a bitch come for me

Set it off, if a nigga come

Bryson Tiller was singing, and the Glocks were now locked and loaded. This shit was really about to go the fuck down. Khalil was maneuvering his Charger through the downtown traffic, switching from lane to lane. The urgency of the situation had us riding on this nigga in our personal car, and that right there showed me how much Khalil wanted this nigga gone. Hassan had given him all of the information we need on the cat. All the way down to the hotel and the room. We parked in a dark alley and walked to the exit of the hotel. Khalil had something to keep the emergency alarm from going off, and we snuck into the back of the hotel with ski masks on. I was still in my high heels from prom, but you wouldn't be able to tell the way that I was keeping up with Khalil. We took the stairs as we made our way to the third floor. Room number 350 was at the end of the hall as soon as we exited the staircase. He picked the door quietly being careful not to make a sound.

Once the door was finally unlocked, he pushed the door opened just enough for us to slide through the door. Once we were inside we closed the door quietly. As we walked in, I could see a trail of clothes leading to the entry of the suite. When I walked into the room, I got the shock of my life. Never in my wildest dreams did I ever think I would ever see the sight before me right now. I looked at Khalil, and he was already looking back at me. I knew the look on my face said it all. Here was my best friend of 11 years riding the nigga that was a lifelong friend of mines, but even worse somebody who once tried to be with me. Granted Deon was never my man fully but before Khalil came along, he was the only nigga I fucked with that heavily. The feeling of betrayal was an understatement. How the fuck could she find the audacity to do this shit to me. I've had this girl's back through all kinds of shit, and this was the fuckin thanks I got.

The shit was blowing the fuck out of me right now, and I didn't know what the fuck to do. My emotions were getting the best of me, and I was losing it on the inside. When bitches tried to warn me about what type of person she was, I ignored them and still was her friend. Hell, the only friend she ever had beside her sister. I was fucked up about the situation because clearly the bitch had been playing under me this entire time. I just couldn't understand for the life of me what would make her do this to me out of all people. Out of all the niggas she could have fucked with she chose Deon. If I had to be totally honest, he would always hold a special place in my heart, but I just didn't feel the way about him that he did about me. That was the reason I could never go all the way through with trying to make us an official thing. That still didn't give her the right go behind me and deal with him. That shit was wrong on so many levels.

Now it was making sense to me. When I heard the girls in the cafeteria talking about it, it all made sense now. I thought to myself, and all I could do was shake my head. The both of them were fucking scum bags and were beneath me. If the both of them were on fire right now, I wouldn't pour a cold drink on their asses to cool them down. These motherfuckers betrayed me in the worse way, and this was something that I would never forget. Being so caught up in my emotions and everything that I was feeling at this moment I lost track of what we were doing here.

Khalil nodded his head, and it was go time. I cleared my throat as I took the ski mask off of my face. Imagine the look on their faces. Autumn turned around, and her eyes were bucked as she looked like a deer caught in headlights. The waterworks started instantly as she looked in my face and tried to cover her body with the sheets. Khalil took off his mask as well, and Deon looked like he could have shitted bricks right about now. His ass was the one who killed JP, so I felt no mercy for what the fuck was about to happen to him.

"Lani ... Lani I'm so sorry. I never meant for you to find out this way, trust me. I never meant to hurt you. You have to believe me, Lani... you're my best friend I love you."

By now I had both of my guns aimed, one at Autumn and one at Deon. My palms were sweaty, and my hands were trembling. I was thinking very irrational at this moment but who wouldn't if they were in my shoes. In a predicament like this, all kinds of fucked up things will cross your mind. Khalil said nothing, but I knew that he knew exactly what I was feeling. That's how in sync we were with one another. Right now, Autumn meant absolutely nothing to me, and I never thought I would feel what I was feeling for her right now.

"Don't come kicking all of that best friend shit to me! You weren't thinking about me when you were just riding this niggas dick like you was on a fuckin rodeo. Bitch, you ain't shit to me, you mean nothing to me as of now and I mean that shit with a passion. Fuck you and this raggedy ass nigga. I never thought I'd see the day Autumn, but you know what shit isn't always what it seems to be. You know you, and I have experienced everything together. You have been my best friend for the majority of my life Autumn, and that's the crazy thing about this ordeal. I looked at you like the sister I never had. Shit's crazy," I said with a light chuckle.

"Lani you don't have to do this shit man. Hell, you didn't want me anyway, look who you here with. This the nigga you chose so I don't even see why you give a fuck about who is screwing me any damn way. I'm sure you're breaking this nigga off on the daily," Deon said, and Khalil let a shot off hitting him in his shoulder.

"Argggggggghhhh!" he screamed out in agony.

Autumn was crying hysterically and begging for her life, but it was going in one ear and out the other. I no longer cared. I already knew what Khalil was going to do to Deon because of what he did to JP. I also knew that Khalil never left witnesses. Quite frankly Autumn was in the wrong place at the wrong time. By now Khalil was done talking, and he was about action. I hated that it had to come down to this, but she did it to herself, she would just be a casualty.

Trust. Something that can be easily broken but not easily earned. It's always the people closest to you that will turn on you in a blink of an eye. Never in a million years did I think I would be standing in a room with my gun drawn on two people that once meant so much to me. In this life, it was either killed or be killed, and I knew for damn sure I didn't plan on dying today.

"If you don't blow this muthafuckas head off in the next two seconds I promise you I will!!!"

I stood there with my guns aimed and my hands trembling like a muthafucka as I moved. I killed muthafuckas on the daily, but right now it seemed like the hardest thing I ever had to do. I was a trained killer and the shit sort of became second nature to me.

The way the two of these motherfuckers

betrayed me, there shouldn't have been a question about ending their lives. I was riding with my nigga right or wrong, and since day one he has proven himself to be the only loyal person in my corner. So, I guess that meant I already knew what the fuck I had to do!

Without another thought, I let off a couple rounds as tears started rolling down my face, but I quickly wiped them away. I just couldn't fathom that I just took the person that I saw as my best friend life. Khalil wasted no time putting a bullet to Deon's dome, ending his life instantly. All of this shit was crazy, and I honestly never saw this coming at all. Today was one of the best days of my life thus far and who would have known that it would end this way. I can't lie it broke my heart that they were gone, but in the end, this was the life I decided I wanted to live with my better half. It didn't matter who they were they had to go. If Autumn would have been the loyal best friend that I expected her to be she would have never been caught up in this shit. But here she was lifeless, lying beside her lover. There was no room for emotion in this game, you had to know how to turn that shit on and off, or you were bound to fuck up.

"Get what the fuck we came for and let's ride Lani!!"

I did what I was told, grabbed the money and the drugs and hauled ass.

Business was Business, never personal.

Getting home that night everything happened with Autumn and Deon was crazy. Khalil knew that I was feeling some type of way, but I couldn't hide it. Even if I chose to he knew me, he would be able to read right through me. We got out of our clothes and had a shower together. I was numb. I felt nothing as Khalil bathed me. I knew that shit was going to hit the fan sooner or later, but it was what it was. I would play my role and act like the heartbroken best friend. In reality, I was because I never expected that type of betrayal from Autumn. I guess I never knew her the way I thought I did. Shit was really crazy out here.

Two days later I got the call that I had been expecting. It was from Autumn's sister Shaunie asking when was the last time that I saw her because she was found dead in a hotel. I played my part so well I could have won an Oscar for my performance. If she was alive, she could have won an award also because her and Deon put on one hell of a show. They kept that shit hidden from me good. Once I got myself together, I got dressed and went to her mama's house where everyone else was. Everyone was torn and heartbroken over Autumn's death and even though I was the one responsible I was hurt too. I didn't want to do that, but I didn't have a choice. Either way, she had to go just for being there if I didn't do it Khalil would have.

Her mom was taking it very hard. Not wanting to drag the process out for a long period of time she had Shaunie go ahead and make the funeral arrangements for next Saturday. I assured them that I would be there with them every step of the way and would assist them in whatever they needed.

***

Today was the day that Autumn would be laid to rest. I never thought that this day would come so soon. It was a rainy eerie Saturday, and the weather matched my mood. Khalil was already dressed, but it was taking me a little while longer to get it together. I put on my black Kate Spade dress with the blazer to match. I had a big black church hat with my natural hair pressed underneath. I wore my black, red bottoms. After putting on my dark shades and spraying my perfume, I was as ready as I was going to be for the funeral. I hadn't heard anything about Deon's funeral arrangements just yet, but I was sure that it would be taking place soon. We met everyone at Autumn's parent's house before heading to the church. Getting in the lineup with everyone we were now on our way to the church. Khalil and I rode in complete silence.

We walked into the funeral right behind Autumn's mother and sister. It was a sad occasion as we walked in and her mother was having a fit as we approached the casket. When Khalil and I arrived there, I stood there for a minute and just looked into her face. She looked at peace. Khalil held my hand the entire time, and we proceeded to take a seat on the pew. The preacher preached a nice sermon, and the service didn't last long at all. I was grateful for that because the whole scene was making me feel light-headed.

Standing at the burial site, everyone stood there silently as we listened to the pastor say one last prayer before dropping her casket into the ground. I could have sworn I saw Shaunie look at me funny, but I dismissed it. I knew like hell she didn't want any smoke because I could surely grant her that wish. We went back to their home for the repass, but we didn't stay long because I was tired and feeling like I needed to lay down. On our way home Khalil took a detour and stopped by Hassan's to check on him and get our money. I was too tired to get out, so I waited in the car until he was finished.

He didn't waste any time in there before he was coming out. We made one more stop by the dollar store to get saltines and crackers. I didn't know what was wrong with me, but I just wasn't feeling too good and I all I wanted was my bed. When we made it home, Khalil helped me out of my clothes, and I just had my cami and underwear on. I got in the bed and snuggled up with my covers. Khalil joined me and just massaged my entire body, it was much needed. Eventually, I dozed off into a deep sleep.

Chapter 19

SHAUNIE

Losing my sister was one of the most devastating life events that I ever had to endure. I felt like half of me was gone, like I lost myself. This was something that I just couldn't shake no matter how hard I tried. My best friend was gone, and life just wasn't the same without her. We had been inseparable since day one, she was my little sister, and we'd always had each other's backs. Even though we had different fathers that didn't change the love we had for one another. We loved each other unconditionally.

None of this was making any sense to me. Especially the fact that her and Deon got killed side by side. I knew that it was something up between them, but she never actually came out and told me straight up. When he came through on prom day, the same day that they were killed, I knew then that whatever they had going on was something serious. We had warned her before about what she was doing wasn't right, but she led us to believe that she had everything under control. My mama wasn't accepting the fact that she was gone at all and it was a hard pill to swallow for all of us. We never did tell Lani that they were caught together when they were found dead in the hotel room. I just felt like if that was something that she didn't know before their passing I wouldn't be the one to tell her.

For some odd reason though the strange feeling came over me that she already knew what was up with them. The more I thought about their deaths it confused me. Autumn didn't have any enemies that I was aware of. It could have easily been she was caught up into some bullshit that Deon had going on, but I just wasn't sure. None of this was sitting right to me. But one thing for sure is that I wasn't going to rest until I find out what happened to my sister. That was a promise. I was going to be looking into this and get to the bottom of it all.

Everywhere I went I was hearing people saying

that they were sorry for my loss. Though I appreciate their prayers and kind words it was only a reminder that she was gone. I knew that we had still had to press through and continue to live our lives. It just wasn't an easy thing to do. Some days I wake up crying and go to sleep crying. Memories that my sister and I shared flooded my mind. I smile when I think about all the good times we shared. We used to have so much fun together; it was so hard to believe that she was gone. I would never forget my little sister, my heartbeat.

Firing up a black and mild in an effort to help ease my pain. I was riding around the city with no particular destination in mind. I just wanted to get out of the house for some fresh air. I had been confiding myself to the four walls in my room and our house for the last couple of weeks. I was tired of sulking in emotions. Staying inside only forced me to think about Autumn more and more. Everything reminded me of her, and that made me hurt even more. My phone had been blowing up lately, but I really haven't been in a mood to talk to anyone. I had over one hundred unread text messages.

I ended up on the south side of town. My homegirl Reese was out sitting on her patio, so I parked the car and went to join her. She got up from where she was sitting to greet me halfway.

"It's good to see you, Shaun, we all have been worried about you. You know since the passing of your sister. We all miss her."

"I appreciate it, Reese, the shit is just hard you know. After all of the crazy shit, I have done out here in these streets I always thought I would be the one to go before Autumn."

"Life just has a way of unfolding, and we never know how the pieces will lay. We just have to take things for what they are and accept the things we can't change. That's just how life goes."

I was listening to everything she was saying as I nodded my head and continued to get my smoke on. Everything Reese was telling me was right, and I needed to hear it. Her kids had come outside once they noticed I was out there. They loved me, and I loved them just as much. We sat outside and talked shit as we watched the kids play in the yard. I didn't notice that

Reese's baby father Carl was in the house until he came and stood at the door.

"What's up Carl?"

"Not shit, how you been Shaun?"

"I'm making it, just taking shit one day at a time."

"I feel it, that's all you really can do. But yo, let me holla at you for a second."

In the back of my mind, I was wondering what the hell he could have possibly wanted to talk to me about, but I went to see anyway. He walked to the side of the yard, and I followed him trying to see what was up. He fired up a blunt a took a pull from it before offering me a smoke, but I declined.

"You know I'm not the one to gossip or anything, but it's word out about who pulled that shit on your sister and that nigga Dee."

"Okay and nigga?! Spit that shit out!"

"Word is that her best friend may have played a part in that shit. Some bitch named Ronni or some shit like that."

"You mean Lani."

"Yeah, that's the name. They say she was sought leaving the hotel room the same night all of that shit happened. Word is that Autumn left the prom in her car. I don't know how true that shit is, but you know how the streets talk. I just wanted to put you up on game sis."

"I appreciate it bruh, I had a feeling that bitch knew what was going on. The shit all makes sense now, once she found out about them she retaliated and now my little sister wasn't here but trust me there would be hell to pay behind this shit. She took my sister's life and now hers will be ripped away."

"Just think rational in all this, don't go getting yourself into some shit that you will later pay for. If anything, have somebody else to do your dirty work if you get my drift."

I was grateful as hell that Carl came to me when he did and confirmed every last suspicion that I was having. I knew that I wasn't crazy and the feelings that I was having towards Lani was accurate. The nerve of that bitch to even show up to my sisters' funeral pretending to be the hurt best friend. There were some conniving people out here in this world. Granted my sister was one but she didn't deserve to have her life taken from her.

For what? All behind a no-good ass hood nigga. The shit was never that deep; hell Lani was in a relationship with that nigga Khalil. I just couldn't understand her motive. It was shocking because I just couldn't see Lani doing that shit, but I guess looks could be deceiving. I knew that she wouldn't have the heart to do the shit, so I knew she had that nigga behind her giving her the motivation to go through with it.

I had to do something about this. I wouldn't feel right knowing that this bitch was still walking and breathing, and my sister was in her resting place. Her and her nigga had to go, and I wasn't wasting any time doing so. I had some cash stashed away, and I didn't give a fuck I was putting a whole brick out on their heads. Them motherfuckers had to go if that was the only thing that I could do to revenge my sister's death then so be it.

Chapter 20

KHALIL

Everything was just starting to get back to normal. Lani was feeling better and was getting back to her normal self. That shit with Autumn and Deon took a toll on her. I think what fucked with her the most was the fact that she thought that she could trust her. In the end, it was all about loyalty, and some people had no sense of the word. That shit was real out here but not too many abided by it anymore. No one was to be trusted in these streets, and it was always the ones closest to you that would turn on you in a blink of an eye. I always knew in the back of my mind what type of bitch she was, but Lani loved her so much that I just couldn't bring myself to tell her.

Seeing them together was something that I didn't expect either. It was clear as day that a relationship had been established between them and it wasn't something that just happened out of the blue. I know that it hurt Lani to the core to have to take her out but either way, it was going to be done. She was just in the wrong place at the wrong time, so she reaped the same benefits he did.

Tonight was supposed to be a pretty night ,so I decided to take Lani out since she was in much better spirits and I wanted to keep it that way. She was getting dressed so that we could go out on the town. Of course, I was always ready before her because my baby was extra. She had to make sure she was looking good from head to toe. I was used to it by now. When she was finally ready, we kissed my mama goodbye and left the house. I made us reservations at a nice little restaurant downtown called D'Road Café. It was both of our first times at the restaurant, so I was decided to try it out. We didn't mind trying new things and creating new experiences together.

When we got to the restaurant, I told the host that I had a reservation for two. He seated us right away. The restaurant was already packed, and I preferred a window seat, but unless we wanted to wait another hour or two, we just settled for a booth in the back. I wanted to make tonight as pleasant as possible. Not wanting anything to throw Lani back into the funk that she had been in lately. I just wanted her to enjoy our time together tonight. We haven't had the chance to do anything together in a while, so I wanted to cherish this moment. The food at the restaurant was spectacular, and I wanted to thank the Chef personally. After we had dessert we left the restaurant and started to walk in the direction of the riverfront. We just walked and talked as we held hands. Lani had a smile on her face, and it made my heart warm. I missed seeing that beautiful smile on the regular.

It was a lot of couples out enjoying the pleasant night air. The Biscuits were having a baseball game, and they must have won because fireworks started going off. I held Lani tightly from behind as we watched the fireworks go off. It was beautiful, and it was the icing on the cake to our night. After they were done, we headed in the direction of the car because I was feeling like going home to make love to my woman. We were both rushing to the car because we were hot and ready like a little caesar's pizza. We giggled as we made our way to the car like little junior high kids anxious to get it on. I pulled off, and I be damned that a red light didn't catch us. I was rubbing on Lani thighs and between her legs when the smell of smoke consumed my nostrils as we sped off from the light.

"Do you smell that?" Lani asked me.

"Yea, I do, where is it coming from?"

"I don't know Lani."

Smoke was coming from under our feet and started clouding the car. We were coughing and trying our best to breathe. As soon as I tried to open the car door the doors and locked and I couldn't get them open to save my life. I could see that Lani was losing consciousness and I could feel myself slipping away as well. The next thing I heard was a loud boom, and I knew then that all of the things that I had done, all of the niggas I had killed had finally caught up to me. Damn man, I never expected to go out like this.

Epilogue

JJ

Hear I was lost in this world feeling like I had nothing left. My sister and Khalil were gone, and all Ms. Connie and I had left were each other. So much had happened these last few months I just didn't know how much I could bare. Even though Ms. Connie and Khalil just established a relationship not too long ago; I knew his death still broke her heart. They had become so close in such a short period of time. He was the big brother I never had. Since the day he came into my sister's life he had the both of our backs, and I would never forget how he was always there for the both of us. One thing that I knew was that he loved my sister unconditionally. The things that he did for Lani showed that. He was a real man, and I aspired to treat my woman just how he treated my sister when I grow up. I would never forget Khalil and everything he taught me along the way.

My sister Khelani, that girl was my world. I

KELSI MCMEANS

loved her with my whole heart. She was more than a big sister. Losing our parents at an early age forced her to grow up before time and care for me. She cared for me the way that a big sister should. She always had my back and was there for whatever I needed. Whether it was help with schoolwork, offering encouraging words, feeding me, clothing me, anything she was there. I will always remember all of the life lessons she taught me.

I was so thankful for the cat by the name of Hassan. He informed that he was a friend of my sisters and Khalil. He told me that Khalil worked for him. Since they have been gone, he has been looking out for Ms. Connie and me. He covered all of the funeral expenses and made sure that everything was nice for us. I appreciated him more than he knew because I didn't have the money to cover it even though I wanted to make sure that they had a proper homegoing. It was a double funeral, but it was closed casket.

Due to the car explosion, Hassan encouraged me to do so. Not really wanting to see what was left of them I agreed. We had pictures blown up of the two of them and that was the way I wanted to remember them. With vibrant smiles and so full of life. The funeral was very intimate and small because neither of them fooled with anyone.

It had been four months now and it all still felt fresh to me. I still had been doing good in school as I knew my sister would have expected me to. Lani was a straight A student, and I was following in her footsteps. Ms. Connie had got her a plant job to help cushion us just in case Hassan decided he could no longer foot the bill. She always made sure I had money for my meets if I had to travel out of town. All we had was each other, and we made sure to look out for one another. Hassan invited us on a family trip with his family out of the country to Cuba. Ms. Connie saw it as a way for us to clear our heads and a chance for us to have a little fun. School was out for summer break, so I figured why not. He was paying for everything, so I felt it was the least that I could do.

Ms. Connie and I had our bags packed, and we were on our way to meet Hassan and his family and their private jet. We all boarded the jet and was in the air headed to Cuba. This was my first time traveling out of the country, so I was excited. I loved to sightsee. Ms. Connie was in a great mood as she made small talk with Hassan's wife. I loved to see the smile on her face because I knew that this was what Lani and Khalil would have wanted. I decided to get me a nap on the rest of the flight. When I woke up, we was in the most beautiful country I have ever laid eyes on. I loved the states, but this was a different ball game. Beautiful palm trees that reminded me of trees in Florida. The buildings were giving me an 80's vibe. I was loving this, loving their culture. I couldn't wait to get out to see all that Cuba had to offer.

Hassan owned property in Cuba. He had multiple buildings that he owned. We were in Trinidad, and it was beautiful, scratch that beautiful was an understatement. I wish that I could live here permanently. We arrived at the building that we were going to be staying at. The butlers grabbed our bags for us, and we entered the house. Hassan pulled Ms. Connie and me to the side and told us he had a surprise for us. I was thinking to myself that he already had done enough for us. He asked us to follow him, and we did as we were told, confused as to what was going on now. We walked through a hallway, and I could see doors open that lead to a balcony. As we turned the corner, I saw a woman with a head full of curly hair. I couldn't see her face because her back was turned towards us. There was a man standing in front of her with a big beach hat on and her hair was blocking his face.

"I want y'all to meet someone," Hassan said to us.

When the woman turned around my jaw dropped, and tears immediately started falling from my eyes. It was my big sister right here in the flesh and Khalil also. This feeling was so surreal for all of us. I never thought once that maybe they were still alive. We had been mourning their death since the day of the explosion. I thought that I had lost both of them for life and I was trying to find ways to cope and go on with life. Now I didn't have to because my bro and sis was right here with me. Lani hugged me, and we were so caught up in our emotions as everyone was reuniting. I was so teary-eyed, but I saw clear as day the big bump in front of Lani.

"You're pregnant Lani, I'm going to be an uncle," I said as tears continued to fall.

All of this was overwhelming, but I was grateful that all of us were here to this day. I was forever thankful for Hassan; this man was a blessing sent from God. He was really family and has shown us where his loyalty lied. This man had all of our backs like our very own guardian angel. They told me how the car did blow up, but Hassan had got word of Shaunie supposed to been getting someone to put a bomb on Khalil's car. By the time he made it downtown, he saw that the car had already caught on fire. True enough that was something they weren't supposed to make it out of. Hassan had some of his boys with him, and they used fire extinguishers to help die down some of the fire to get access to the door. They busted the window and pulled them both out as quick as they could. They suffered from minor burns and were honestly lucky to be here today. That was all thanks to Hassan and the good man up above.

My sister was five months, and Khalil Jr. would be here in the next couple of months. My family was back together, and I was ecstatic. This was the way it was always supposed to be. My sister and I had been through a hell of a lot but in the end she got the man of her dreams, and they were expecting their first child. Khalil and Lani had eloped in Cuba and have been married for three months.

The love between Khalil and Lani was inevitable, and when she finally let that wall down and let him in, she welcomed in someone who loved her through all of her faults. Their love was untainted. I guess this was the type of love you invite into your heart when you had it bad for a Hitta like Khalil.

The End

CPSIA information can be obtained
at www.ICGtesting.com
Printed in the USA
LVHW041820100419
613666LV00002B/107